A Feast Most Foul

~A Court of Mystery Novella~

Book Two

Sarah E. Burr

Other books by Sarah E. Burr

The Court of Mystery series

The Ducal Detective
A Feast Most Foul
A Voyage of Vengeance
A Summit in Shadow
Throne of Threats
Paradise Plagued
Burdened Bloodline
Sovereign Sieged
Crown of Chaos
Harrowed Heir
Ravaged Reign
Innocence Imprisoned
Ardent Ascension
Eternal Empire

More Cozy Mysteries by Sarah

Trending Topic Mysteries
Glenmyre Whim Mysteries
Book Blogger Mysteries

www.saraheburr.com

A brief history…

Centuries ago, the corrupt and powerful priests of the Ancient Faith lorded over the continent. Poverty and sickness ravaged the world, forcing a faction of rebels to rise up and overthrow these tyrants preaching in the name of silent gods. The leaders of this movement, known in the annals of history as the Rebirth, proclaimed the realm would no longer answer to nameless demons and gods, but to the virtues of bravery, humility, kindness, and intelligence. Under these Virtues, the world would once again flourish. Sealing their pact, these newly anointed leaders drank the dew of the fabled kingsleaf flower, ensuring their offspring would be marked as the divine protectors of this new era with their royal eyes.

Welcome to the Realm of Virtues.

The
Realm
of
Virtues
The
Brave Sea
Lysandeir
Cetachi
Pettraud
Kuatalar
Mensina
The
Sea of
Intelligence
Crepsta
Saphire
The
Sea of
Humility
Zaltor
Beautraud
Tandora
Festes
Savant
The
Kind Sea
Isla
Delacqua

Chapter One

Her head pounded abruptly on the window of her carriage, jolting her awake. Looking around in a daze, she wearily noticed the change in the landscape surrounding her. No longer did her amethyst eyes reflect the rolling hills of her beloved Saphire, but the sprawling plains of Mensina, the dukedom ruled by her austere grandfather. Outside, she could hear the chatter of the ducal guards accompanying her royal procession, each man sounding truly excited to be included in this matter of ceremony. Had any of them been traveling with her inside the carriage, she doubted even her bleak mood would burst their youthful bubbles of joy.

Leaning back against the soft, cushioned headboard, Jax stared up at the intricately carved ceiling. This trip churned a whirlwind of emotions inside her. With her parents' murder a mere few months ago, the Duchess thought she'd finally started coming to terms with the betrayal uncovered by investigating their deaths. But as she rode down the same path they planned to travel that fateful day, her wounded heart began to bleed once more. Her grandfather had given her ample time to recover, or so his courtiers curtly explained, and was now requesting her presence at the Feast of Champions to recognize those who competed in Mensina's Tournament of Virtues. A tourney her parents set out to attend all those weeks ago, but instead, lost their lives.

Jax was still quite annoyed that her grandfather demanded she attend this ridiculous event primed with pomp and circumstance, just to support his duchy. She hardly thought her presence mattered, but he was insistent that her appearance at his ducal table would put to rest any doubts about her resolve to rule. Jax smirked as she remembered forcefully reprimanding the trembling courtier delivering the lecture. There were no doubts concerning her ability to reign as Duchess of Saphire, seeing as how the duchy continued to prosper under her rule and survived its most recent scandal. Word of her benevolent leadership spread throughout the Realm of Virtues, cementing her high esteem with the other nations.

Considering she had not seen her mother's family in nearly three years now, Jax doubted this would be a welcoming family reunion. Bitter that her grandfather continued the Mensina tourney after learning of his eldest daughter's death, she'd pouted the entire journey at the thought of being civil toward him. He didn't even have the decency to send a representative to her own coronation, for virtue's sake. Why should she go out of her way to make him happy? She had yet to figure out why he had extended her an invitation to the Feast of Champions at all. What did he care if Saphire was thought of as weak with her at the helm? Wouldn't that pave the way for the duchy of Mensina to rise in the ducal rankings?

Her top suspect surrounding the sudden invitation trotted outside her carriage with her guardsmen. Lord Pettraud, the seventh son of the Duke of Pettraud, was her formal suitor, and their prospective marriage posed potential issues for the other duchies. It was no secret Saphire was the leading duchy in the realm, and with an unmarried woman now on the throne, there was a chance to control Saphire through her hand in marriage. She had no doubt that her grandfather would present a Mensina man, probably a distant cousin, to try and usurp Duke Pettraud from getting his hands on Saphire's power. Little did her grandfather, or even Duke Pettraud, understand, but Duchess Jacqueline Arienta Xavier was no one's puppet. She and Perry had a mutual fondness for one another, and the Duchess suspected that one day she could grow to truly love him, but she would not allow her duchy to be taken from her and ruled by other men. Perry knew this, and respected her more for it. Her duty was to her throne and her people. She would not lead them astray—not after everything her father had done to ensure his dukedom reigned supreme.

Closing her eyes, she pictured her parents, her father's handsome face, boyish and lively, and her mother's, regal, beautiful, and immaculate. She saw so much of herself in them. Her mother's honey-colored hair and high cheekbones, her father's pristine purple eyes, the mark of a ducal line. She missed them dearly. She had never been in the presence of her formidable grandfather alone, and she was not looking forward to the experience without her father by her side. Her grandfather held the old-world view that a duchess was simply not as competent as a duke. His degrading comments broiled in her mind. "A woman's place is beside a man, never where he stands." Groaning, she remembered a winter's feast from her childhood when her grandfather berated her for entering the room before one of his sons-in-law. "But why, Grand-Père?" she'd asked. "I am to be a duchess, and he is nothing!" Oh, how she'd been punished for that remark. She did not receive any presents during the celebration, except for the ones her father secretly left under her pillow.

A tap on the window jolted her from her reverie and Captain Solomon's strong, attractive face appeared before her. "Your Grace, we shall be arriving at the palace in about an hour or so."

Although the prospect of seeing Duke Mensina made her cringe, she smiled with genuine appreciation for her most loyal ducal guardsman. She was grateful he hadn't insisted on staying behind to watch over the duchy. This being her first visit abroad since her coronation, she felt particularly on edge and wanted people she could trust around her. She would be on display for the entire world to see, and after the assassination of her parents, she still felt very vulnerable to an attack. Captain Solomon made sure his best men were left in charge of the Saphire, and High Courtier Jaquobie, her royal advisor, was left to oversee the day-to-day administration in her absence. She did not want to be gone long, but her grandfather insisted she stay the full fortnight of the festival. "A time to get closer to your family, my dear. They are all you have left now," his courtiers said. Jax's stomach rolled at the thought. What family? The Mensina were virtually strangers to her, having shipped off their eldest daughter to marry the son of the wealthiest duke in the realm. Since their marriage and her subsequent birth, Jax remembered only a handful of times when she'd seen her mother's kin.

Pressing powder to her travel-worn face, Jax looked jadedly at the vacant seat before her, where a lady-in-waiting normally accompanied their sovereign. Jax had yet to select a replacement to fill the position, gladly taking on the responsibilities herself. The help of her maid Uma, who traveled in the carriage behind her, was all the help she needed, or wanted, for the meantime. As much as it mortified Jaquobie that the Duchess of Saphire would be traveling without a lady-in-waiting, Jax just didn't have the heart to replace her beloved childhood friend Aranelda. She doubted she would ever be able to find anyone to fill the role, and decided weeks ago that rather than settling for someone she didn't fully trust, she would do without for the time being.

A short while later, Jax heard the creaking welcome of the

Mensina gates, opening to allow their party entrance into the lively city. Curious to see the state of the capital, Jax eagerly peered out the small carriage window, but was careful to keep her face hidden from the townsfolk. She wasn't quite ready to be gawked at just yet.

Much like Sephretta, the capital city of Saphire, Mycenia was a bold display of the power Mensina held across the realm. When she was a small child, Jax remembered her paternal grandfather, the Duke of Saphire, and his constant lament, "Never trust those who want your power for their own." He often spoke of the marriage between his beloved son and Lady Amaryllis, the eldest of Duke Mensina's daughters, regaling how the trickster planned to use his own daughter to manipulate her new husband and take Saphire for his own. Yet something happened that Duke Mensina did not anticipate; his daughter fell in love and put her husband's duchy before the one of her birth. Lady Amaryllis eventually confided in Jax's father and grandfather about Duke Mensina's desires, and since then, Mensina has been kept at arm's length.

The Duchess could see now, as she gazed at the cobbled streets and bustling markets, that imitation was the sincerest form of flattery. It had been a few years since she'd been to Mensina, and she hardly recalled it looking eerily like her own nation. The Duke must have been busy cultivating his empire in the new era of globalization her own father had introduced to the realm.

The late afternoon sun caressed the red clay rooftops, drawing Jax's attention to the impending skyline. While no other palace rivaled the grand castle of Saphire, she couldn't help but be impressed by the lofty towers rising into the sky, a beautiful silhouette in the peachy sunlight. In a flash memory, Jax reminisced climbing to the top of one of those towers to spy on the handsome guardsmen in the courtyard, with Arnie by her side.

With a heavy sigh, Jax smoothed her burgundy skirts, waiting for the luxurious carriage to roll to a stop. She made sure that every aspect of her traveling party reflected the wealth and power of her duchy. Her royal guards were adorned in new gold and purple tunics, her carriage recently renovated with gleaming jewels and gold accents, and she had an entirely new wardrobe, courtesy of Monsieur Duval, her personal tailor. Lastly, she had ensured that only her most glorious crowns were brought for the various ceremonies and parties. The simplest of them sat on top of her honey-colored hair now, glittering in the natural light of the fading day. It was pure gold with three amethysts embedded into each swooping point; the gems chosen for how well they highlighted her imperial amethyst irises— the mark of a true ducal blood line.

Captain Solomon's warm, common-born brown eyes greeted her through the window. "Your Grace, it appears your grandfather is waiting to receive you," he stated formally, but the concern in his gaze told her what she needed to know. Her grandfather planned to meet her out here in the open, to let the realm gawk while he greeted his estranged granddaughter with feigned affection. Rarely did a Duke ever meet guests face-to-face, unless they wanted to make a show of it for some political reason or another. She would need to be cautious.

"He looks ever so welcoming." Lord Pettraud's handsome figure appeared at her carriage door, his arm extended in reverence to her. His dark hair was unruly from riding horseback, but he still looked as beautiful as the day she first laid eyes on him. His lavender eyes crinkled with suppressed laughter as she nipped at him to shut his mouth. Perry was forever getting himself into trouble by speaking his often-inappropriate mind, and she begged the virtues that he did not embarrass her in front of her daunting grandfather.

"Perry, please remember what Courtier Jaquobie instructed. Around my grandfather, it's better if your mouth remains closed," Jax hissed under her breath as she demurely stepped out of her carriage.

"What, am I here as just a pretty face, then?" Perry asked with mock indignation.

"Yes." Her eyes flashed, already cursing him for distracting her from making a smooth entrance. The last thing she needed was to be seen bickering and reprimanding her intended consort.

She heard shuffling from behind her wall of guards, and saw a horn rise into the air. "Presenting Her Illustrious Highness, Jacqueline Arienta Xavier, Duchess of Saphire," a voice boomed, as if projecting all around the courtyard, trumpets heralding her arrival.

Her sentinels marched in front of her, a wall barricading her from any surrounding eyes, even those of her grandfather. Beside her as they walked arm-in-arm, Perry snorted at her title, remembering the first time he'd heard her called that. "Is that a real thing, then?"

Jax couldn't hide a smirking chuckle. "I think it makes me sound rather important, don't you think?"

"Why not 'Her Divine Magnificence'? Now, that has a quite the ring to it."

Jax comically pondered. "You know what? You just might be right. I'll have to send word to all the courtiers in the land to make sure I'm announced as lavishly as possible." Her response caused the two of them to dissolve into giggles, their attention diverted from the parting of her Ducal Guard.

"My, it is so lovely to see my granddaughter smiling in light of all the tragedy that has befallen her recently." A gritty, deep voice cut through the air, sending a chill down Jax's spine. Her eyes trailed up the steep steps ahead of her delegation, an imposingly broad man looming down from the top. Wiry gray hair was tamed by a gaudy crown, dark violet eyes staring right into her soul.

"Greetings, Grand-Père. It is delightful to be in Mensina once more," Jax responded, not addressing her grandfather by his proper title, nor giving him a bow. She and Jaquobie had planned for days how she was to receive her family, and they decided that reminding her grandfather of his place in the realm was the best move to show Saphire's constant strength.

The flash of anger she saw in the elderly man's eyes told Jax she'd hit a sore spot. Nevertheless, she ascended the stairs like a graceful cat, opening her arms for a stiff, unpleasant hug. If anyone had been watching them closely, which most people in the courtyard were, they would have hardly noticed that the two ducal rulers barely touched one another.

Turning her attention to those gathered around them, Jax searched the crowd for familiar faces. "Ah, my lovely aunts," she exclaimed with genuine affection, for her mother often spoke fondly of her four sisters. The youngest, Amia, petite and fair, was only a few years older than Jax. She came forward from the crowd first to kiss her niece on each cheek. Adelaide and Adella, taller and striking dark-haired twins, greeted her warmly, followed by Annette, her mother's closest sister.

"You look so much like our dear Amaryllis, Your Grace." Annette wistfully stroked Jax's cheek. Nearing forty years of age, Annette looked like the ghost of her mother. Both had the same straight, delicate nose, luscious honey tresses, and high cheekbones. Although looking at her now, Annette seemed to have an air of contentment about her, where her mother had an air of cool superiority.

"You're too kind, Lady Annette. I wish you could have visited for the funeral." Jax couldn't help the bitterness that laced her words. Her grandfather's grudge against her father seemingly prevented any family members from being at the public memorial as well as her subsequent coronation gala.

At the sensitive remark, Amia's eyes flared up toward her father. "Believe me, dear niece, we wish we could have been there as well."

Keeping her face neutral, Jax inwardly celebrated. She was heartened to know that her aunts were not in agreement with Grand-

Père's decision. "Well, I'm thankful that we have this time to catch up with one another, now that I'm here." Giving Amia's arm a reassuring squeeze, she turned back to the Duke. "Have the festivities formally begun, Grand-Père?"

He cringed again at her use of his pet name, but ushered her inside the palace foyer, away from the prying eyes of ducal staff working in the outdoor gardens. "There are a few delegations we are still waiting for, but House Mensina will kick off the feast this evening with a special joust. We are encouraging all knights to partake in the entertainment."

She felt Perry straighten beside her. "That sounds delightful. I'd like to nominate Lord Pettraud to represent Saphire, since none of our knights remained for the full length of the tourney." Her words were cool, as she remembered issuing the order to summon the Saphire knights back to their duchy following the untimely deaths of their Duke and Duchess. She had been shocked to learn upon their arrival home that Duke Mensina refused to abort the tournament, hence Saphire placed last in the standings. "I believe Lord Pettraud took home a few trophies when he was here."

Duke Mensina didn't even meet her gaze, turning his full attention to Perry, his beady eyes inspecting every inch of her future consort. "Ah, yes. Lord Pettraud won a few medals in the cross-country rounds. A brilliant rider, if I recall."

Surprised that her grandfather opted for flattery, she saw her companion flush dangerously with pride at the Duke's compliment. Despite her stern warning, Perry broke his silence and bowed to her grandfather. "I am delighted to be here, sir. It is an honor."

Barely acknowledging Perry's greeting, Duke Mensina turned to his daughters and motioned for them to accompany him inside. "My steward will show you to your rooms, Jacqueline. I shall see you at dinner." With that, he marched swiftly through the palace doors, his long red cloak trailing behind him.

In his place, a tall, stick-thin man appeared from the shadows, dressed in fine silk clothes that hung awkwardly from his slender frame. With a balding head of hair, and greasy beard, he reminded Jax of a weasel. His nose twitched, as if he smelled something sour, his expression condescending as he approached her. "Your Grace, if you will please follow me, I will show your delegation to your guest apartments in the southern wing." His haughty tone assaulted Jax's eardrums, making her fume.

"Of course, Master Steward. Lead the way," she replied with equal arrogance, Perry stifling a snort behind her as the Master Steward led the Saphire group from the courtyard into the bowels of the castle. She found herself continuously rolling her eyes at the gaudy, ostentatious decorations that littered the corridor walls. Her grandfather seemed to be fond of the naked human form, considering how many de-robed statues she counted along the way to their private wing.

"The Duke requests your prompt arrival at the jousting tourney this evening. I shall be back to collect you at six to escort you down to the arena." With hardly a bow, the Master Steward turned on a shiny heel and clomped languidly away.

"He's quite the character," Perry surmised from the door of his chambers, watching the slimy man disappear down the long hall.

Jax frowned, not remembering this odious man from her previous stays. "He must be new to his position. He hardly seems to know how to properly address a Duchess." She pursed her lips in disapproval, wondering why her grandfather kept such a pompous man around.

"Your Grace, shall I prepare a bath for you?" Uma emerged from the small room she claimed, adjacent to Jax's apartment.

Jax smiled gratefully. "That would be wonderful, Uma. You always know just what I need." Uma had been her private maid since she attended the Academy, which felt like ages ago. Quiet and reserved, she made the perfect companion, always in tune with what her Duchess needed without Jax having to ask. "But make sure you leave enough time for yourself to get ready. I've arranged for you to attend the evening's events."

At this, Uma's eyes brightened with excitement. Since the passing of her parents, Jax tried to make more of an effort to include Uma in her life, outside of mere servant work. Uma had been incredibly faithful to her, and Jax wanted to repay the woman's kindness by letting her have a little fun.

Clearing his throat, Perry saluted his goodbye as he closed his door. "I'll let you ladies have at it. I'm going to rest up a bit."

As soon as the young lord's door clicked shut, Jax motioned to Captain Solomon, who was standing duty near the south wing entrance. "George, I want you to make sure Lord Pettraud does not leave his room unattended and go wandering off. The last thing I need is for him to meet someone and run his mouth without my supervision."

Chuckling at her familiarity, Captain Solomon rolled his eyes. "Jax, he's a grown man. He can take care of himself, you know."

Giving the captain a severe look, Jax pleaded once more. "Please, at least for tonight. I don't want Saphire making the wrong kind of splash." She knew she could just order her ducal guardsman to do what she wanted, but considering her close friendship with George Solomon, she hoped he would do it without protest.

"I'll assign him an escort for the night. Although I'm sure my men would rather be enjoying the celebrations themselves," he said with a sigh, making Jax feel slightly guilty, but not enough for her to change her mind.

"I'll treat them to a pitcher of mead tomorrow, then. Just make sure he doesn't stick his foot in his mouth and cause trouble," Jax quipped before shutting her door with finality. Leaning against the frame for support, she surveyed the apartment her grandfather had reserved for her. Much smaller than her quarters at home, she frowned as she noticed dust covering much of the space. Obviously, this was Duke Mensina's move to put her in check.

Fortunately, Uma made swift work of filling the porcelain tub and Jax lowered herself into the calming bath waters, her mind replaying the events of the afternoon. She wasn't sure where it came from, but she'd seen a devious spark in her grandfather's eyes that made her feel uneasy.

Chapter Two

Uma outdid herself putting together Jax's ensemble for the evening. Looking at her trim figure in the mirror, Jax's own breath caught as she admired the stunning mint green ball gown, dripping with golden jewels. Her honey hair was gathered up into a regal pile of curls, a decadent crown sitting amid her tresses. With expertly applied makeup that heightened the intensity of her eyes, Jax knew no one would dare question her authority as a ducal ruler. "Excellent work, Uma. I hope you saved enough time to get yourself ready. I must meet the Master Steward now, but I shall see you later in the evening." Smiling warmly, Jax floated out of her room and into the hallway.

Perry stood at attention, wearing the traditional Saphire knights' ceremonial wear and a rather anxious expression. Preoccupied with his thoughts, he didn't notice Jax's presence until she was right beside him, at which time his eyes nearly popped out of his head. "My goodness, you look striking."

She coyly twisted a ringlet of hair. "Why, thank you, Sir Knight.

I see you are prepared for the joust." Her eyes flicked to the dazzling sword hilt protruding from under his cloak.

"Well, someone signed me up for this without even asking. I thought I was going to have a relaxing evening."

His words surprised her. "I'm sorry, Perry. I thought this would be something you'd enjoy." She fidgeted under his gaze, crestfallen that she'd disappointed him.

His stone face broke into a grin. "Only joking. My escort and I did a bit of surveillance in the Great Hall. The knights are already sloshed off their faces, so my pristine frame of mind should give me quite the advantage."

Jax's face blushed at Perry's implication. He obviously knew she was having him monitored, but he chose the high road and did not pester her about it. "I'm sure you'll represent Saphire well."

A sadness appeared in his eyes that she was unable to account for. "I plan to, Your Grace."

Before she could pry further about his sudden change in mood, the Master Steward arrived, beckoning them to follow. "I will escort you to the ducal box at the arena, Duchess Jacqueline Arienta, and then deliver Lord Pettraud to the jousting grounds." The man instructed in a wheezing voice. Jax made a face behind his back, catching Perry's eye. While the steward reminded her of her own High Courtier, Jaquobie, the man slouched before her was much slimier and more revolting. Why her grandfather had appointed him to such a position of power, was beyond her.

She was grateful, however, to have someone lead her through the winding maze of palace walls and out into the gardens toward the tournament arena. Even though she had visited Mensina a handful of times in the past, she was no expert at navigating the imposing fortress. Mensina was known for its state-of-the-art showground, frequently the duchy of choice for tournament games. She could see a horde of tents pitched all around the arena, each bearing the flag of a visiting duchy. She assumed this was where most of the knights attending the Feast of Champions made camp during their stay. Jax was one of few awarded the honor of staying in the palace for the fortnight, or so Duke Mensina's courtiers liked to remind her. She would have laughed in their faces if they seriously believed she would even consider staying in a tent.

Surveying the rows of campsites, Jax lost count quickly. "Looks like you'll have some competition this evening, Lord Pettraud," she commented formally, mostly for the benefit of the Master Steward slinking ahead of them.

She saw Perry's gaze sweep the fields, nodding mutely. She frowned, wondering if his quiet behavior was due to nerves. Rarely had she ever seen him looking anything but joyful. It troubled her. Perry was her ray of sunshine; she hated seeing anxiety on his face.

Seeing a flurry of motion to her right, she caught sight of her grandfather being carried down to the grounds on a royal rickshaw. Her initial thought was indignation at not being offered the same courtesy, being made to walk instead. Not that she minded, as she'd been cooped up all day in her own carriage, but the affront was still blatant disrespect on her grandfather's part. The second thing she noticed was that the old man looked incredibly displeased. She suspected he was angry about something. Hitching up her skirts, she quickened her pace and raced past her sputtering guide. "Grand-Père!"

With a sharp look over his shoulder, he barked his driver to halt. "Not now, Jacqueline. I have an urgent matter to attend to."

Reaching his side, with Perry close behind, she rested her hand on the arm of his carriage. The Duke was agitated, which alarmed her somewhat, for he was not a man to lose his composure. "I can tell something's wrong. My mother always got the same little furrow on her forehead when she was upset."

Perhaps it was the mention of his departed first child that caused her grandfather to sigh with strangled emotion. For a moment, he rubbed his temples, his gray hair getting in his way. "It's nothing to concern you. I wouldn't want to dampen the evening's events for you."

She slowly moved her hand off the carriage and clasped Duke Mensina's trembling fingers, the most intimate gesture she'd made toward him since she was a child. "It does not seem like nothing, Grand-Père." Her curiosity burned bright, her mind churning.

Looking at her through his dark violet eyes, he grimaced as if in physical pain. "I just learned that one of my messengers was killed on his way back from delivering an invitation to the Feast of Champions."

While shocked to learn of the death, it surprised Jax that the news affected her grandfather's hard heart so greatly. "What happened? Was he attacked by Cetachi rebels?" Her mind went immediately to the wild men living in the ungoverned, swampland province. The rogues were forever causing chaos across the Realm of Virtues, trying to overthrow the ducal system.

Duke Mensina huffed at her unfounded conclusion. "Oh goodness, no, child. Don't be ridiculous. The royal physician said he was stabbed by a unicorn. The horn went right through the poor boy. He was barely fifteen."

"A unicorn?" Perry spoke up, sounding confused. "Why on the virtues would a unicorn kill the lad?"

Jax turned to her suitor, knowing that he had never encountered a unicorn in the flesh before. "It probably got spooked and charged at him. While they are beautiful beasts, they are still wild and dangerous."

Duke Mensina shifted in his seat. "I must deliver the news personally to the boy's father. He's a member of my private ducal guard. I shall see you in the box, Jacqueline, and you on the field, Lord Pettraud." With a whistle, he signaled his carriage to resume its journey.

Jax watched him disappear into the rowdy crowd swelling ahead of them. "That's terrible. His poor family."

"Not the best omen for the festival, either," Perry mumbled, resting a hand on the hilt of his sword. "Makes me not want to see a unicorn as much anymore, for certain."

Nodding in agreement, they continued down the path toward the arena, the Master Steward introducing them to delegations from other duchies along the way. Jax noticed she was the only sovereign among the invited nations; the other duchies had sent their knights alone on their behalf, accompanied by a courtier or two. She growled inwardly, knowing her presence was merely a stunt to promote her grandfather's standing in the ducal order. If he could be seen alongside his granddaughter, the Duchess of Saphire, it would raise his ranking among the other leaders, especially after the distance her late father had put between Mensina and Saphire over the years.

The Master Steward made good on his word and delivered her first to the royal box in the grandstands of the arena. It was positioned high above the field, but in dead center, giving her the ideal view to watch every aspect of the action.

"I'll be watching you with rapt attention," she teased Perry, her laughter dying on her lips as she caught sight of his pensive expression. His lavender eyes scanned the fairgrounds, but the alertness was clouded over by something she couldn't quite identify. "Perry, is everything all right? You seem out of sorts." She waved a hand in front of his face, drawing his focus back to her.

"I suppose I am still a bit worn out from our journey, that's all," he mumbled, absently grasping the hilt of his sword.

His lame response troubled Jax. Obviously, he had something more pressing on his mind, but with the Master Steward watching them from the shadows, she decided not to press him further. Bidding goodbye and good luck to her preoccupied knight, Jax entered the seating area to find a few of her aunts already present with their husbands. Adelaide and Adella sat together in the front row of regal chairs, while Amia sat in the back of the space with a gaggle of children surrounding her, whom Jax guessed were her young cousins.

Adelaide noticed Jax first, her mouth dropping open. "Jacqueline, you look breathtaking, my dear. The knights won't be able to concentrate on their jousting when they see you."

Smirking, Jax glanced down at the gathering crowd finding their seats in the arena. "I think Grand-Père had the Master Steward parade me around the grounds for that very reason."

Amia's head snapped up. "Reginald made you walk down here? What game is he playing?" She pushed herself off the ground, brushing her beautifully tailored yellow dress free of wrinkles.

Glad to have a name to put to the unpleasant steward, Jax gave her aunt an exasperated look before making her way to greet the husbands in the room.

As she approached, the men bowed in unison, their bright amber eyes gleaming, a symbol of their noble pedigree. Jax thought all her uncles looked the same, mostly because they came from the same bloodline. The Lacosta family was one of the wealthiest noble houses in the region, and when it became apparent Duke Mensina could only get his first daughter married off to a Duke, he chose his daughters' suitors based on their ability to contribute to the ducal treasury. Amia and Adella's husbands were brothers, and Adelaide was married to a Lacosta cousin, which accounted for the brood of children who all looked eerily alike in the back of the room. "It's good to see you all." She held her hand out to each of her uncles for a kiss, trying to remember their names, but failing miserably. She'd been twelve the last time she'd seen them. She didn't even try to engage with the children, fearful that their messy hands would ruin her gown.

Taking a seat next to her grandfather's arena throne, she

surveyed the field with calculating eyes. Knights from all over the realm were filing in on armored horses, most looking like they regretted starting their celebrations so early in the day. "Is this expected to take long? I'm famished." Jax placed a hand on her growling stomach, perturbed that her grandfather hadn't sent any food to her rooms.

Adella took a seat behind her, giving a small chuckle. "You haven't changed a bit, dear niece."

She was about to repeat her question, in need of a response, when Duke Mensina entered the box, scowling darkly. He likely had just returned from giving the news of the page boy's unfortunate demise, so Jax chose to keep her mouth shut. Reginald slinked in behind her grandfather, giving Jax a sour appraisal.

"Take your seats, everyone. We're about to begin." Duke Mensina barked the words to his daughters, their husbands obediently scampering to the remaining chairs. With a flick of a finger, a trumpeter was signaled, and a horn cried for silence over the grandstand. "Citizens of Mensina and revered guests! Welcome to the Feast of Champions!" Her grandfather's voice carried heartily throughout the stadium, his gruff appearance melting into that of an endearing host. "Over the next fortnight, we shall celebrate and honor the knights who triumphed at the Tournament of Virtues. For your entertainment, these knights have returned to the arena for a joust. The winner of tonight's event will be the Master of Champions and have the privilege of dining at my ducal table." Looking down at the assembled sea of men, the Duke continued, "in the name of the Virtues, let the best man win!"

With her amethyst eyes, Jax searched the crowd, hoping to spot Perry. Sighing in disappointment, she could not find the purple-and-gold garb of Saphire amongst the group, so she sat back and watched the game unfold before her. Knights were paired against each other, the winner of the match continuing to play until just two knights were left in the arena. It was a sloppy mess for the most part; Jax could practically smell the mead from her seat. It wasn't until there were five pairs left on the field that she finally recognized Perry. Instead of the purple and gold knights' tunic Monsieur Duval designed for him, he wore the colors of Pettraud.

"I thought Lord Pettraud was representing Saphire in tonight's event?" her grandfather mentioned slyly from his seat next to her.

I did too. Inwardly, Jax seethed, but gave the Duke a sweet smile. "Our grandmaster armorer unfortunately made Lord Pettraud's neck piece a bit too snug, so we opted for the more mobile choice." Figuring it was better to throw her armorer under the carriage rather than admit her ward's blatant disrespect for her duchy, Jax smoothly brushed the conversation off her shoulder. She would have a word with Perry after the joust.

Amia leaned forward from the second row, whispering in Jax's ear. "Lord Pettraud is quite adept at this. I remember him performing well in horsemanship during the Tournament of Virtues. I didn't realize he was a skilled fighter. No doubt, he will make it to the final round against the Knight with No Face."

Jax turned her head around, giving her aunt a confused look. "The Knight with No Face?"

Grinning like a lovesick schoolgirl, Amia giggled. "He's the representative from Beautraud, a legend in the arena. He's won over seventy contests in his day."

Jax searched the crowd, hoping to catch a glimpse of the warrior. "Why do they call him the Knight with No Face?"

"When he's in competition, he is never seen without his helmet on. He eats in secrecy within his tent, so that none of his opponents will know who he is. There are very few people in Beautraud that even know what he looks like. His whole career has been shrouded in mystery." Amia's face reflected her childish delight as she offered the rapid explanation.

Jax looked down at the field, her eyes locking on the knight clad in the black-and-yellow armor of Beautraud, a southern duchy in the realm. "Well, how is he going to participate in the feast? With his helmet on the whole time?"

From the corner of her eye, she saw her grandfather's mouth lift with smug triumph. "We received word from his delegation yesterday that the Knight with No Face plans to announce his retirement this very evening, taking off his helmet to reveal the man beneath."

Amia gave a breathless sigh. "It's going to be the talk of the realm."

Jax sat back in her chair, her curiosity piqued. Mensina was no doubt counting on the fame and notoriety of the Knight with No Face revealing himself to the world at their feast. And if the knight was as elusive as Amia claimed him to be, Mensina could very well upset the balance of power in the realm with this little exploit. While her own duchy was secure in its ranking, she feared for her closest allies, Pettraud and Crepsta. If either felt their power shift or crumble because of this stunt, they might blame her for sitting at her grandfather's side. Despite Amia's glee at the entertainment aspect this Knight with No Face provided, Jax's stomach flipped with slight worry.

"And now, our final round. Our champions, Lord Pettraud representing Saphire and the Knight with No Face from Beautraud!" An announcer's voice rattled Jax from her thoughts, her eyes drawn to the scene below. Sizing up the two men, Perry certainly appeared to have the upper hand in size and mentality. Like so many other knights on the field, the legendary Knight with No Face was knackered. He must have been a skilled warrior to make it this far in the competition considering the drunken state he was in.

Duke Mensina must have realized his champion's state of mind, as well, for Jax caught his lips tightening in boiling anger. It would certainly take the wind out of his sails if the Knight with No Face failed to perform well.

The joust was over quickly, Perry delivering one direct blow to his opponent, the man landing flat on his back in a puff of dirt. Jax rose to her feet and clapped eagerly for her champion, relishing the sound of his name announced as the winner on behalf of her own duchy. Turning to leave the grandstand box, she paused in a manner befitting her title and thanked the Duke of Mensina for the pleasant event, making a point to claim her grandfather's one-person rickshaw for her journey back to the palace.

Chapter Three

Her amethyst eyes scanned the crowds of men and women marching their way up to the castle for the feast, keeping an eye out for Perry. To her growing disappointment, he was nowhere to be found. Wondering if he had gone to change back into his Saphirian attire, she urged her driver onward until he pulled the rickshaw to the base of the palace steps. All eyes were on her as she gracefully floated up the stairs and through the entrance, murmurs of her beauty buzzing through the crowd. But her ears also detected an undercurrent of whispers, speculation about the deaths of her parents and her own safety. Jax knew the immediate threat to her life had been eliminated, but it was not something highly publicized. She felt ashamed of the betrayal she had been so blind to, so she buried the conspiracy as best she could.

"Your Grace, might I escort you into the banquet hall?" Captain Solomon appeared at her side, he and his men returning from both guarding her and watching the joust.

"Your presence would be welcomed, Captain." Jax slipped her

arm through his and they walked through the parted sea of people. "What did you think of the game?"

Captain Solomon chuckled. "I'd hardly call that a joust. Most of those men could barely stand, let alone fight. I will say I was impressed with Lord Pettraud, however. He was ruthless, not backing down an inch."

Jax searched the crowd for her suitor, to no avail. "Yes, he was quite something," she murmured, mostly to herself, as they stepped into the banquet hall, lined with dozens of long tables, each piled with food and wine. With the huge chandeliers flickering light overhead, it was an impressive sight by any standards. In her short tenure as Duchess, the largest group Jax hosted had been a hundred guests for her coronation. Duke Mensina appeared to be expecting well over three hundred. "Is one of your men still with Perry? I've lost track of him." She surveyed the room once more, with no success.

"Yes, Jax. Someone will shadow him all night, until he retires for the evening." George grunted at her precautions. "I don't think he's the one you need to worry about this evening. Your grandfather is in quite a sour mood."

"I don't think he was impressed by the final performance of this mysterious Knight with No Face. Apparently, we're in for some big reveal tonight." She waved her hands with a dramatic flourish, tugging a chuckle from her escort.

"We mustn't dally then." Captain Solomon motioned her through the myriad of tables, leading her up to the platform where the ducal table waited. She was the first to arrive. Her grandfather was likely planning an elaborate entrance with his other family members in tow. It did not bother her that she wasn't included. She preferred to have a quick moment alone, overseeing the entire goings-on in the room.

At the blaring assault of a trumpet, those gathered struggled to stand at attention, waiting for their sovereign and host to make his appearance. Jax remained firmly seated in her chair, turning her head to the wings where she saw her grandfather's looming shadow.

"Ladies and Gentlemen," a courtier's voice echoed from atop a balcony, "may I present our gracious host for the Feast of Champions, Archibald Horatio Pendleton, Duke of Mensina."

A thunderous applause followed as her grandfather walked purposefully to his seat at the long table, his four daughters in his wake. Amia, Adella, and Adelaide all sat beside their husbands to the left of her grandfather, and Annette took a chair on Jax's right. Her beloved husband had died only a few months into their marriage, and as far as Jax knew, Annette made the choice not to remarry, a wish that Duke Mensina uncharacteristically granted. She remembered her mother sharing the news of Uncle Aaron's passing, devastated at her darling sister's heartbreak. "Don't marry for love, Jacqueline. It's more trouble than it's worth." To this day, Jax wondered if her mother had been talking about Annette's heartbreak or her own, for her mother lost touch with her family by choosing to honor her husband over her father.

"Your Lord Pettraud will be joining us, yes?" Annette whispered into her ear. "He won the right to sit at the ducal table."

Jax shot a glance at her grandfather, who seemed to be intentionally ignoring her, even though their elbows nearly touched. "I suppose that honor must be offered by our gracious host," she replied coyly, loud enough for the words to tickle Duke Mensina's ears.

As if on cue, Perry appeared before them, dressed in his untarnished Saphirian tunic. "Your Excellence." He bowed, not addressing Jax, but the Duke.

Begrudgingly, her grandfather rose and cleared his throat, silencing the grand hall. "It is with honor that Mensina invites Lord Pettraud, the Master of Champions, to the ducal table." At his sweeping gesture, a chair appeared to the left of his throne, skillfully placed by an invisible servant.

Stone-faced, Perry climbed up to the ducal table and took his seat, his profile barely visible to Jax. She imagined it was her grandfather's calculating idea to separate them, on display in front of his entire duchy. Annette either saw the look of annoyance on her face, or guessed what she was thinking, for she felt her aunt give her arm a comforting squeeze.

With Duke Mensina monopolizing Perry's time, Jax settled into an enjoyable conversation with Annette, each sharing the goings-on of their respective lives. Even when she was younger, Jax preferred Annette's company over that of her other aunts. She was a woman of substance and intelligence, where the others seemed superficial and shallow.

"Oh boy," Annette mumbled through a mouthful of chocolate soufflé. "Get ready for a show."

Jax followed her gaze to the center of the room, noticing the Knight with No Face, still in full armor, making his way toward the front of the ducal table. To her left, her grandfather stiffened to attention, placing his goblet on the table with a commanding thud. While the Knight with No Face had not won the Feast of Champion's jousting match, he remained a revered warrior, or so the hush in the room told Jax.

At last arriving in front of the Duke, the Knight with No Face bowed low, his black and yellow tunic brushing the ground. "Your Excellence, may I have the floor?"

Jax rolled her eyes at the request, for the entire room was already eating out of the masked man's palm, the silence almost unnerving.

Duke Mensina stood, his shadow casting down upon the knight. "You may, Sir Knight." Crossing his arms, he looked expectantly at the warrior.

The Knight with No Face turned to the room, his voice liquid gold as it captured the attention of all. "Greetings, brave knights and esteemed courtiers of the realm. I have had the honor of representing Beautraud for the past seven summers as their champion, traveling all over the world to compete on their behalf. I come before the Duke of Mensina and his ducal table tonight to formally pass my mantle to my successors back in Beautraud, for I am officially removing my helmet."

A gasp washed over the room, eyes widening and mouths hanging open. From her vantage point at the head of the room, Jax could see that this news was entirely unexpected. Whatever intelligence her grandfather had received about the knight's retirement was indeed a well-guarded secret.

Milking the announcement for all its worth, the Knight with No Face slowly reached up behind his helmet and lifted the silver mask off his face. The guests couldn't seem to decide if silence or a low murmur was warranted as the man revealed himself publicly for the first time.

Jax's initial thought was that it was a shame a face that gorgeous had been hidden from view for so long. The Knight with No Face swept flowing gold locks away from his tanned, chiseled cheeks. A sharp, straight nose heightened the intensity of his amber eyes, the indication of his noble birthright. The knight turned around, giving the whole hall a quick glimpse at his stunning good looks. At last, his gaze rested directly on Jax, bowing once more. "Let me introduce myself as Sir Antoine Wincaester of Beautraud."

Jax felt her face flush at the intensity of his stare, as though the man saw into her very soul. With a shifting look up at her grandfather, she noted his grim expression. He was not pleased with the attention being paid to her. "Welcome, Sir Antoine of House Wincaester. We honor you this evening." Duke Mensina raised a glass, bringing the stunned room back to life. "Please, join us at the ducal table."

Another chair appeared, this time at the far end of the table, next to Amia's husband. It seemed her grandfather was determined to keep Sir Wincaester as far from her as possible. Jax smirked, knowing that the influx of guests seated to her grandfather's left made the ducal table look lopsided and unsightly.

As the famed knight ascended the stairs to the high table, Jax watched the other guests cram and strain their necks to try to get a good look at the man. With the amount of drink being consumed in the room, she mused that Sir Wincaester would likely need to reintroduce himself in the morning, for everyone's vision was no doubt a bit fuzzy by now.

Instead of heading directly to his seat, Sir Wincaester rounded her side of the table, stopping mere inches from the back of her chair. "I wanted to personally introduce myself to the fairest face in the room. It is the highest honor to be in your presence, Your Grace."

She felt his breath on the exposed skin of her shoulder. Turning her head ever so slightly, her regal eyes met his hungry gaze. "You are too kind, Sir Knight."

His eyes darkened with mischief, and he took her hand, kissing it ever so seductively.

Next to her, Duke Mensina grunted a fake cough, pulling the knight's attention to his host. "Thank you for your generous invitation to join you at the ducal table, Your Excellence," Sir Wincaester said cordially, "I could not have dreamed of better company for the remainder of the evening." With that, he sauntered off to the end of the table where he immediately engaged in lively conversation with her aunts and uncles.

Watching his muscular frame swagger away, Jax felt another flutter in her stomach. She smiled to herself as she turned her focus back to her desserts, feeling giddy from the obvious flirtation.

"Quite the suave man, is he not, Lord Pettraud?" Duke Mensina's voice commented dryly.

"It would seem so," Perry's voice was emotionless, his

expression cool as an embarrassed Jax met his disapproving gaze. What kind of spell had Sir Wincaester put on her to make her entirely forget her suitor a few feet away?

She felt Annette's body shift closer, her whisper barely reaching Jax's ears. "Be careful around that one, love. Men like that are always trouble."

Chapter Four

Jax woke with a start the next morning, her dreams quickly fading into oblivion. Unsure of what spooked her out of unconsciousness, she surveyed the room with bleary eyes. Uma scampered around quietly in the corner, laying out a beautiful floral gown for Jax to wear during the first full day of the Feast of Champions. Uma, noticing her charge was awake, smiled politely and bowed her head. "Greetings, Your Grace. Your grandfather has requested your presence at breakfast as soon as possible." Her pale cheeks flushed with embarrassment, clearly uncomfortable delivering a secondhand reprimand to her sovereign.

Rolling her eyes with a flourish, Jax lazily pulled herself out of bed. "Pay no heed to my grandfather's threats, Uma. He does not control me, nor you, for that matter." She yawned as she assessed her outfit for the day. "You truly are gifted with such style, my dear," she praised her faithful maid, causing another round of blushing. With skillful hands, Uma tied the Duchess into the dress' built-in corset, then fashioned her hair in a long, intricate plait, a silvery crown tucked into her shining tresses.

"You look lovely, Your Grace. I'm sure Sir Wincaester won't be able to take his eyes off you." Uma's lips tightened ever so slightly in jest.

Whipping her head around meet her maid's chocolatey gaze, Jax huffed. "What in the name of the virtues have you heard? Is there really gossip already floating around the castle?"

Uma bit her bottom lip, breaking their connection to stare off into the distance. "Well, it seems Lord Pettraud had some choice words about Sir Wincaester's 'charms' when he retired to his room for the evening, or so his valet reports."

"Good grief, is that so?" Jax gathered her skirts, feeling indignant. After the indifferent way Perry had regarded her yesterday afternoon, she was surprised to hear his jealousy come forward. She was in all but a binding contract with his father, Duke Pettraud, concerning their marriage. Why did he feel the need to complain about another's flirtatious affections? She hardly batted an eye when women fawned over him, so why should he when the situation was reversed? "It appears Lord Pettraud must have let the wine and mead go to his head last night. He was clearly imagining things. Sir Wincaester merely paid his respects to me."

Uma giggled unceremoniously. "I didn't say anything about Lord Pettraud complaining about Sir Wincaester's charms toward you, Jax."

The use of her familiar nickname pulled a smile from the Duchess's lips, knowing she'd been caught red-handed. "No, you didn't, I suppose." In times past, Uma would not have dared address Jax with such familiarity, but Jax was trying to break down the gap between servant and master to one of true friendship. "All right, this former Knight with No Face may have flirted a bit too much, but it was all in good fun."

Opening the door to the private apartment, Uma gave Jax a meek look. "From what the valet said, it didn't seem like Lord Pettraud took it all that lightly."

"Thank you for the warning, dear one." Jax gave her a squeeze. "I'll sort it out over breakfast."

‡

Jax entered the banquet hall a few moments later, disappointed that Perry was nowhere to be seen. She still needed to speak with him about his stunt with the Pettraud tunic during the joust. He'd skillfully avoided conversation with her last night, so she was determined to sort out whatever was going on between them. She wasn't used to being at odds with him.

Her grandfather sat with Adella and Amia, their husbands conversationally bantering on about the festival's events. At her arrival, they all looked up and greeted her.

"Ah, Jacqueline, how did you sleep?" Duke Mensina asked with strange mirth in his eyes.

"Quite well, Grand-Père, thank you." Jax sat down with hesitance, trying to assess the mood of the room.

Her grandfather took a sip of tea. "How about Lord Pettraud? Was his apartment suitable? His valet failed to make mention of it to my staff."

So, there it was. Duke Mensina had obviously heard about Perry's outburst over Sir Wincaester and was poking around to see what damage had been done. "A fine substitute for his suite back in Saphire," she replied, her words dripping with sweet sarcasm, lost on everyone but her grandfather. She saw the triumph in his face, this round of their power play going to him.

The doors swung open behind her, and she turned, expecting Perry to enter. Her smile faded slightly when she laid eyes on Sir Wincaester. Sauntering over to the long table, he winked at her as he

40

took a seat opposite her, looking incredibly well-rested after the night's drinking. As he stared at her expectantly, she struggled to make conversation with the dashing young man. "What a surprise to see you here, Sir Wincaester," she finally announced, "I would have thought you would be down at the festival grounds with the rest of the common folk."

Chuckling, the knight brushed his glowing hair out of his face. "Please, Your Grace, I insist you call me Antoine. 'Sir Wincaester' makes me sound much more important than I really am." He winked at her giggling aunts. "The Duke invited me to stay in the palace for the duration of the feast. I believe I am only a few suites down from you." His eyes twinkled with flirtation.

Restraining herself from throwing a peevish look at her grandfather, Jax merely blotted her lips with a silk napkin, feigning disinterest in the knight's attention. She could practically feel the heat of his gaze on her bare skin, a sensation that she both loathed and welcomed at the same time. She chided herself for these adolescent thoughts. What was coming over her? Was she so desperate for affection that she was succumbing to this rogue's charms? Where was Perry? She closed her eyes, praying her rightful suitor would appear by her side.

"Besides, now that I am retired, I felt a bit out of place among the men last night." Antoine took a long sip of sparkling juice, looking around the room to ensure he had everyone's attention. As she listened to his bravado, Jax could hardly believe a man with this big of an ego had managed to keep his identity a secret for so long. "I heard them from my chambers here in the palace. It sounded like things got quite rowdy."

"Well, you put a hundred hot-headed men together and things are bound to get boisterous," Duke Mensina chortled, clearly enjoying the dynamic his latest guest brought to the room. "I hope that even though you have retired, Sir Wincaester, you will join us when we ride out for the hunt this afternoon?"

Raising his glass, Antoine tipped his head in gracious acceptance. "Of course, I could never pass up the chance at bagging myself a prized Mensina stag."

Jax's stomach flipped. She had forgotten about the hunt, its aim being to gather all the meat for the remainder of the festival. Women typically did not partake in the event, but since she was visiting as a foreign dignitary, it would be prudent for her to saddle up and accompany the men. Luckily, under Perry's tutelage, she'd grown into a more strong and confident rider since he'd come to stay with her. Thinking about his skills in horsemanship, she looked around the room and was shocked to see Perry hunched over at the end of the long table, talking to one of her uncles and Reginald, the Master Steward. When had he entered the room? Was he avoiding her? Had his pride really been so wounded by Sir Antoine's attention?

Just as she was about ready to call down to the end of the table and claim his focus, a flurry of activity out in the hallway startled the breakfast guests from their conversations. Captain Solomon and a man who appeared to be the captain of the Mensina guard appeared at the door of the banquet hall, their shoulders tense. "Your Excellence," the Mensina captain said with a bow, "might I have a word in private?" His tone did not indicate the Duke had a choice to refuse an audience.

She met Captain Solomon's fevered stare, a quick jerk of his head ushering her away from the table. Bidding a hasty goodbye to her dining companions, Jax strode down the long table, passing Perry with a concerned glance. "George, what's all this about?" she whispered as the captain took her by the arm and guided her to a small, windowless chamber where they could talk in private.

"There's been an incident down at the campgrounds, Jax. A man was found dead in his tent this morning."

His words chilled her, and her hands clasped tightly together.

"What happened?"

George ran a callused hand through his dark hair, looking tired. "At first it appeared that the man might have died from a bad heart or from too much drink. His comrades said he was pounding the mead quite hard toward the end of the feast last night. However, once Captain Roche ordered him to be removed from the grounds and brought up to the castle for examination, the court physician found a small wound in the man's back, which appears to have punctured his heart and lung. He practically drowned in his own blood."

Jax brought a hand to her mouth, stifling a gasp. "What a terrible way to die. How did this happen?"

"We went back and searched the tent to see what we could find. It's not good, Jax." George's face was lined with grim worry. "We found a slim dagger that fits the physician's assessment of a murder weapon."

"Murder? Goodness, George, are you sure?" Jax's breath caught in her throat.

Captain Solomon nodded gravely. "There's no way it could have been self-inflicted. But that's not the worst of it, Duchess."

Jax's eyes widened as she hung on the captain's every word.

"The dagger bore the crest of Saphire."

Chapter Five

"How in the name of the virtues did one of our daggers get into this man's tent, George?" Jax hissed at the implications.

He looked at her uncomfortably, unsure how to proceed. "All my men's weapons are accounted for, Your Grace. The only person traveling in our delegation that we have not yet searched is," the captain trailed off, his eyes pleading with the Duchess to figure out the rest.

"Perry." Jax felt her insides freeze as she made the connection. "Perry was given a set of ornamental weapons before we left the palace. He was instructed to use it for ceremonial purposes when we attend formal dinners." Jax remembered handing him the sword and knife, a coy smile exchanged between them at the time. "I gave it to him myself. I could verify if it is the same one you found."

"And if it is the same dagger, Jax, do you know what this means?" George asked, his voice soft.

She gave him a harsh look. "It means nothing conclusive, Captain. Perry changed for the jousting match down at the fairgrounds yesterday. Someone could have easily stolen his blade before, during, or after the match. I'd like to think our Lord Pettraud would be smart enough not to leave a murder weapon that clearly identifies him at the scene of a crime."

Captain Solomon scrutinized her intensely. "You think he is being set up?"

"I think I need to find my grandfather before he jumps to conclusions and does something he'll regret. I'm assuming the Captain of the Ducal Guard has the knife on his person?" Jax gathered her skirts to leave the room.

George nodded. "Yes, Captain Roche was going to show the Duke and fill him in on the events."

"Wonderful. I bet the two of them are conspiring against me as we speak. Can't your men account for Perry's whereabouts last night? I instructed that he be accompanied by a guard at all times." Her eyes narrowed dangerously on her captain.

"As we both agreed to last night, Perry's chaperone escorted the young lord to his chambers after the feast and retired from there. My men confirm that the order was carried out." The captain struggled to keep his expression calm under the Duchess's wrathful gaze. It was clear he was at fault for not stationing a guard outside Perry's door throughout the night, but Jax checked herself, knowing she was being unfair. Even she didn't have a guard at her own door here in the Mensina palace. Her grandfather's courtiers repeatedly assured her that the entire guest wing would be well protected by the Duke's men.

Calming her raging nerves, Jax led the way out of the room, her stride brisk and purposeful. Changing the subject, she focused on the matter at hand, not the regrets of last night. "What else do we know about the man who was killed?"

Her captain marched beside her. "Not much, unfortunately. He traveled with the group from Savant, but he had not been in their company long. Apparently, he's a wandering knight who hires himself out for entertainment. He wasn't one interested in the glory of knighthood."

Jax wondered a moment. "His name?"

"Master Chalfant."

The Duchess forced herself to move faster down a long hallway, the memory of her grandfather's tucked-away study guiding her way. "I need you to find out more about this man, George. We must do everything possible to clear Lord Pettraud's name up front before we figure out what really transpired."

"Jax." The captain grabbed her arm gently, pulling her close to conspire. "Are you certain that Pettraud didn't have anything to do with this? It would not be wise for us to defend a man without having complete confidence in his innocence."

Jax ripped her arm away with irritation, her voice cold and low. "Yes, Captain, I am certain that my intended consort did not sneak away and murder a man last night."

If the head of the Saphire Ducal Guard was intimidated by her seething, formidable response, he did not show it. Instead, he drew himself up to his full height and stared down at her with dark eyes. "Might I remind the Duchess that it is not in the duchy's best interest to let emotions and feelings get in the way of logic and reason?"

She opened her mouth to spew a fiery protest, but he cut her off. "As of the conclusion of the feast last night, our Duchess and her Ducal Guard do not have any confirmed reports of the whereabouts of her suitor. The only record of his movements was an outburst from his private chambers, recounted as gossip by a loyal valet from his homeland of Pettraud."

Despite her anger at his disrespectful approach, Jax allowed his words to work their way through her calculating mind. True, she had lost track of Perry at the feast's end, as he skillfully ignored her for most of the evening. For all she knew, he could have gone to celebrate down at the arena with the remainder of the knights. Only Uma's joking remark about the valet verified Perry had returned to his rooms after the banquet. If the valet's story proved false…

"Figure out who the dead man is, Captain. That is a direct order from your Duchess." Her sharp tone concealed her wavering certainty at the warning George issued. He was right, after all. She could not stick her neck out for Perry just yet. She had to know without a doubt he had not done this. "I'm going to find Lord Pettraud and his valet."

"You're out of your mind if you think I'm going to let you go alone," the captain sighed with exasperation.

"We don't have time for this back and forth, George. I need to get to Perry before my grandfather does. Duke Mensina is going to act swiftly for fear of tarnishing the festival's success." Jax left the Captain's side with one final statement. "I do believe Perry is innocent, but I am willing to play by your rules. Now please, go find out what you can about this Master Chalfant." Not waiting for his reply, she scurried in an unladylike manner down the hallway, winding her way back to the dining hall. Slipping in through a side door so as not to draw too much attention to herself, she spotted Perry sitting quietly at one of the plush chairs nearest to her. Without so much as a word, she grabbed him forcefully by the shoulder, dragging him in her wake back into the empty corridor.

At least having the sense to remain quiet until she hauled him to his suite, he waited until the apartment door was firmly latched before raising his hands in bewilderment. "Goodness, what was that about, Jax?"

Seeing his obvious distress, she felt a pang in her heart. She wanted to say a myriad of things. That he had no need to be upset about Sir Antoine and to ask why he was being so chilly towards her. She longed to lose herself in his comforting arms, but she took a deep breath, focusing her attention on the immediate matter at hand.

"Perry, something terrible has happened. You may be in danger. Where is your valet? I need to speak to him immediately."

Her statements registered as nonsensical, his expression confused. "What? Why am I in danger? And what does that have to do with Hendrie? He's been my right-hand man for years." Perry's voice trailed off. His sad eyes exposed the realization that the 'loyal friend' argument was no longer something Jax inherently trusted, due to her recent experience.

She waved his questions aside, her temper flaring. "Summon him here, now, Lord Pettraud."

His skin paled, knowing the use of his proper title meant Jax was gravely serious. With a tug of a thinly veiled cord hanging from the wall, somewhere deep in the castle, a bell beckoned Hendrie to hasten. "While we wait for him, do you care to explain what in the name of the virtues is going on?"

Jax folded her arms across her chest, pacing the length of the well-furnished sitting room. "Last night a man was killed down on the fairgrounds."

"Good grief, how? Was there some kind of drunken brawl?" Perry rushed to her side, clearly shocked when she backed away from him.

"No, Perry. He was murdered. Killed by a dagger bearing the seal of Saphire," Jax held his stunned gaze for a moment.

Lord Pettraud's face reflected a flurry of activity, of which she watched closely. Confusion and shock hurriedly danced across his features, followed by incredulity. "What, and you think it's the one you gave me? That's not possible." He kicked his long, muscular legs into motion, marching over to a sleek row of bureau drawers. "Why, I had it with me last night at the feast, and put it back in this bin when I returned." He slid open the compartment, rifling through its contents. "Wait a minute. It's not here. Jax, it's not here!" He pushed both hands through his tangled dark hair, pulling it back in frustration. "It's not here," he repeated once more, turning swiftly to face her. "I swear to you, I put the dagger in this drawer when I returned from the feast."

Jax tiptoed over and peered inside, confirming that the dagger was indeed gone. "Did you leave your rooms at all last night? Could someone have come in without you noticing?"

The young man stroked his chin, trying to recall his movements from the previous night. "I did go out onto the veranda off my bedroom and have a nightcap with Hendrie. I imagine you may have heard that I got a little defensive regarding Sir Wincaester's playboy behavior."

Jax felt her cheeks blush. "Yes, Uma mentioned it to me this morning. Hendrie was a bit loose lipped with the other servants."

Perry frowned in momentary embarrassment, but seemed relieved by the vindication. "So, yes, I would say someone could have quietly snuck into my chambers without either of us noticing. We were quite rowdy with our own interpretations of the Knight with No Face."

"And Hendrie will confirm this?" Jax prodded.

He looked at her, visibly shocked. "What, you don't believe me?"

Jax gave him a hopeless look. "Perry, I do believe you, but unfortunately, we are at the mercy of my grandfather, and right now, he has a murder weapon that belongs to you. We need concrete proof to ensure he does not escalate things unnecessarily."

"Unnecessarily? You think he'll try to use this to tear down Saphire?"

It touched her that Perry's thoughts went to her duchy first, and not of his own reputation. "I'm more worried about what he could do to you. To you *and* me." Jax lowered her eyes, reaching for Perry's clammy hand. "I told you before we came here that Duke Mensina can be a cruel and calculating man. I wouldn't put anything past him. Now, where is your valet?" She stomped her foot impatiently, panic and hysteria beginning to seep into her calm exterior.

At that moment, a straw-haired, scrawny young man stuck his head through the apartment door, obviously not realizing his charge had a guest. "You rang for me, Perry?"

The valet's candid greeting made Jax's heart ache for that kind of familiarity with Uma.

"Yes, Hendrie, Duchess Jacqueline has some questions for you about last night," Perry motioned for the man to enter, pinching the bridge of his nose as if to ease the tension building up in his head. Only then did Hendrie notice Jax and immediately fell into a pattern of gracious bows.

"Please, Hendrie, no need for royal protocol right now. I need your rapt attention," Jax murmured with the grace of a socialite, capturing the valet's focus. "Can you recall for me, please, what happened last night after Lord Pettraud returned from the feast?"

Hendrie's nose wrinkled in thought, clearly curious as to why he was being asked. "Well, Perry, er, Lord Pettraud came back to his suite around midnight, only a few minutes after the rest of the guests departed for the fairgrounds. I took care of his garments while he readied himself for bed. We ended up having a drink outside on the balcony, for you see, I had found a nice bottle of whiskey in one of the cupboards in the sitting room. It was quite tasty, ma'am. I don't think I got myself into bed until after three." He looked at her openly and unafraid.

Analyzing the man's brown eyes as he spoke, Jax saw the truth in his words, although, she thought grimly, she had been fooled before by those closest to her. However, she was sure the valet's statement would hold up, should Duke Mensina interrogate the lad. "Thank you, Hendrie. One last thing. Do you remember anyone entering the room while you were out on the veranda? Or did you notice anything suspicious in the hallway when you left?"

Hendrie glanced over at Perry, worried. "No, Your Grace, I

didn't. Has something gone missing, sir?" The young man trembled, probably fearful that Jax's line of questioning was about the quality of his service.

"It appears that my new dagger was removed from my quarters while you and I were having that drink, Hendrie. A man has been murdered with it," Perry stated grimly.

"Murdered?" Hendrie nearly choked on his surprise. He looked from Jax to Perry in disbelief.

Jax stepped forward, hoping to soothe the troubled valet. "Yes, Hendrie, and with Lord Pettraud's dagger used as the murder weapon, we'll need you to tell Duke Mensina exactly what you told us to clear his name from suspicion."

"What? The Duke thinks Lord Pettraud killed this man?" Poor Hendrie looked like he was about ready to collapse into tears.

Before Jax could respond, there was a staccato knock on the door, and an authoritative voice grumbled on the other side. "Lord Pettraud, open up. This is the Captain of the Ducal Guard." Based on the way the man's voice creaked with age, it was not George Solomon.

The three exchanged tense looks, Hendrie making his way forward to open the door. The armored man Jax had seen with Captain Solomon at breakfast appeared, her grandfather looming behind in his shadow. "Duchess, I did not expect to see you here." The Duke's voice revealed little surprise, giving way to the lie.

"Hello, Grand-Père. You know me, I had to get to the bottom of things myself, once I heard about Master Chalfant's untimely demise," Jax replied smugly, alluding to her grandfather knowing her history of unraveling any puzzle put before her. "I was just listening to Hendrie's account of the evening's activities. The young lad states he was with Lord Pettraud all night, so of course, we can immediately clear him of any wrongdoing."

Duke Mensina raised his bushy gray eyebrows mockingly. "All

night?" He clasped his hands behinds his back. "Tell me, valet, what time did you depart Lord Pettraud's suite for the evening?"

Hendrie's face turned deathly pale at being addressed by the imposing man, but his voice was steady as he responded. "Lord Pettraud and I were out on the veranda from his return at midnight until around three in the morning, Your Excellence. I left just as he was going to bed."

"Three in the morning, you say?" The Duke stroked his beard with false thoughtfulness. "It should interest you to know," Jax's grandfather said as he turned to meet her square in the eye, their regal gazes burning fire, "that the deceased Master Chalfant was reported being alive until at least four this morning, when he left the gambling tables and returned to his tent. We can safely assume that his death occurred just before daybreak."

Jax felt her heart harden as she watched her grandfather prepare for his elaborate finish. "We also found a torn piece of fabric not belonging to Master Chalfant on a bush right outside his camp. Captain Roche, if you will?" With a waving command, the guardsman swiftly opened a nearby bureau, revealing Perry's wardrobe.

"Excuse me, but what are you implying, Duke Mensina?" Perry burst forward, his face red with rage.

"It would appear," Captain Roche boomed, his voice dripping with disdain, "that this tunic needs mending, Lord Pettraud." He held up a green shirt, embroidered with the royal seal of his homeland duchy. Jax's horrified eyes wandered to the hem of the cloth, where a large, gaping hole fluttered in the air.

"My, my, it looks like we have a match," Duke Mensina sneered with triumph, watching his granddaughter's reaction.

"Lord Pettraud didn't even wear that suit yesterday, Your Grace," Hendrie exclaimed, appealing more to Jax than the Duke.

"It is likely that he changed into it after you left, valet. Your word is hardly valid." Duke Mensina barked, snapping his fingers at Captain Roche to spring into action. The captain lunged forward and seized Perry, whom to Jax's surprise made no moves to protest.

"Anything to say for yourself, Pettraud?" Duke Mensina approached the captive, clearly savoring the moment.

"Obviously you have already made your own conclusions regarding this matter, Mensina, so I have nothing to say to you." Perry's voice was as calm as Jax had ever heard it. "But to Duchess Jacqueline, I ask that she see the truth in my eyes, and find out why I am being framed for a man's murder."

His words kicked her stunned mind into action. "Indeed, Grand-Père, surely you of all people are smart enough to know this is a plot of some sort. A man as decorated and accomplished as Lord Pettraud would not be daft enough to leave behind all this incriminating evidence." Her skillfully chosen words poked at the Duke's ego, and she saw the briefest spark of insecurity in the old man's eyes. "Without any witnesses placing Lord Pettraud at the scene of the crime, you must be forced to consider that this man is indeed being framed. By winning the jousting match, as well as being my intended consort, he would be the ideal target to defame."

Captain Roche and Duke Mensina shared a glowering look, telling Jax they each knew she had them beat with her logic. "While we will not formally charge the lord until the investigation has concluded, I will exercise my right to detain him in the dungeons until I am satisfied with his innocence."

Jax made a move to object, but a small head shake from Perry silenced her. She couldn't let her feelings get in the way of ducal protocol. "Very well. Who is leading the investigation, Grand-Père? I will work with them."

Her grandfather threw his head back, his entire body shaking with laughter. "You will do no such thing, Jacqueline. You are a Duchess. Leave these matters to people who actually understand how to handle them." Without answering her question, he motioned for Captain Roche to escort Perry out of the room, leaving Jax and Hendrie standing there dumbfounded.

Rage boiled through her. She couldn't believe the lack of respect in her grandfather's response, treating her like an incompetent child. "Hendrie, I ask that you relocate your belongings to this suite. I want you to stay in this room and keep watch until we've gotten to the bottom of this mess. Come find me or Uma immediately if anyone other than myself or Captain Solomon tries to enter this room."

"Your Grace?" Hendrie's eyebrows scrunched in confusion, unclear of her intentions.

Jaz responded with a confident nod. "Quickly, now, Hendrie. We've got a murderer to find."

Chapter Six

Jax left a bewildered Hendrie in Perry's abandoned apartment, a hasty plan brewing in her mind. She hoped George Solomon had taken his men down to the fairgrounds to dig deeper into this Master Chalfant's past. Figuring out who this man was would help her get a clearer sense as to why he'd been killed, and why Perry was taking the blame for it.

Upon seeing the torn tunic, she now was completely certain that her suitor was being framed. Perry, always meticulous about his appearance, would never simply leave a damaged piece of clothing without tending to it first. She learned this from Monsieur Duval, her ducal tailor, for he complained often about the surplus of work he now had with Perry living in Saphire. The young lord was always ruining his clothing whenever he rode horses or trained with the ducal guards, leaving it in the care of the tailor immediately afterward. Monsieur Duval may not have accompanied them to Mensina, but as a guest of the Duke, Perry had access to the palace seamstress, and as Duval frequently commented, "That man would have me sew up his shirt first if he had an arrow sticking out of his chest."

She felt somewhat ashamed of being more convinced by the torn clothing item rather than Perry's own pleas of innocence, but as Captain Solomon reminded her, she could not let her personal feelings obstruct her reasoning. While she did not want to admit it, she was terrified by the fate that awaited Perry, now at the mercy of her grandfather. Her stomach flipped at the thought of her intended trapped in the ducal dungeons. She had to figure this whole scheme out before the Duke did something vengeful. The one small beacon was that the Duke knew he needed to be cautious with the handling of this investigation, for the powerful duchy of Pettraud would not sit idly by and let one of its sons be unfairly prosecuted. Her words had put enough doubt in her grandfather's head that he needed a motive to formally charge Perry.

The walk to the courtyard seemed endless, but soon Jax felt the sun caressing her face as she stepped out of the shadows of the palace. People were idly milling about the gardens, allowing her to catch snippets of conversation as she marched purposefully along. Most of the talk was about the upcoming hunt, something that completely slipped her mind in the chaos of the eventful morning. She was not looking forward to riding beside her grandfather after their face off, but she knew he would take it as a surrender if she did not show up.

The large clock tower tolled eleven, warning her that she only had a few more hours until she needed to be seated firmly in a saddle. Clutching her skirts so as not to trip, she snaked off the worn path and dashed into the woods, avoiding detection, which allowed her to run quickly to the outskirts of the festival campgrounds. While she could hear Courtier Jaquobie's condemning words at her disregard of etiquette— "A *duchess never runs, Jacqueline*" — she knew she had not been seen by anyone as she stepped out of the shady woods and onto the sprawling fields near the arena. She scanned the scene, taking in the numerous clusters of ornamented tents, each looking too luxurious for camping. She had no idea where to begin her search for Master Chalfant's quarters, so she hastened her way toward the makeshift galley, fumes of roasted pig and duck wafting through the air.

Knowing she looked too much like a duchess, her nimble hands grabbed a shabby blanket near a mound of hay and threw it over her shoulders like a cloak. The musty smell hit her forcefully, the essence of horse or donkey tingling her nostrils. Pinching a smidge of dirt between her fingers, she rubbed it furiously on her cheeks, quickly transforming into a tourney wench, a term for wayward women who traveled around with knights for entertainment. Tucking her skirts up to reveal more than a prudent amount of leg, she completed her disguise and rushed toward the eating area. If only Jaquobie could see her now.

"Excuse me," Jax purred in a husky voice to a man stirring a large, bubbling cauldron, "could you tell me where I might find Master Chalfant's tent or someone who might know where he is? I need to tell him about a little surprise coming his way," she crassly rubbed her stomach, making sure not to meet his eyes and give away her royal heritage.

"Off with you now, you strumpet. Chalfant is over on the north side, near the Savant delegation," the galley master said as he waved a steaming ladle at her, thwarting her from coming any closer.

Eager to leave, she gave him a crooked smile and dashed away, nimbly snagging a bumbleberry tart as she departed. Munching on the sweet morsel while she wove her way through the maze of tents and knights, her sharp eyes noticed a familiar face under the Savant banner.

"George!" She scampered over to the captain of her guardsmen, touching his shoulder in greeting.

Startled, he turned to look at her, already pushing her away in disgust until he met her gaze. "Jax! What in the name of the virtues are you doing? Look at yourself!"

His horrified gasps sent her into a fit of giggles. "I had to improvise to make my way down here as quickly as I could. I needed to get down here without being watched," she explained, growing serious. "George, my grandfather has taken Perry into custody. Apparently, Roche's men found a ripped tunic in Chalfant's quarters that matches one hanging in Perry's chambers."

Captain Solomon's brow furrowed. "Lord Pettraud rushes off to Duval the moment he's pulled a thread."

"I know," Jax said with a sigh. "I'm certain he's being framed. Someone broke into his chambers, took the dagger and ripped a piece of the tunic, all before going down to the fairgrounds to murder Chalfant."

"It seems like someone has gone to extraordinary lengths to set up Lord Pettraud. Do you think it's someone looking to sabotage your engagement?" The captain's brow furrowed as he mulled over the situation.

Jax contemplated for a moment. "Possibly. But I think the answer lies more in who Master Chalfant is. If the intent was to frame Perry, they could have picked anyone. Why this particular victim?"

Captain Solomon frowned at the point she raised. "Well, at this moment, I don't have much to report. The Savant knights he was traveling with said the man pretty much kept to himself. He was quite wealthy for a knight of his caliber. Apparently, Chalfant participated in farcical tournaments rather than real ones."

"Farcical tourneys?" Jax's nose wrinkled with unfamiliarity.

"Jousts and fights that are laden with comic relief. Often, the men dress up in outlandish costumes and the knight who makes the crowd laugh the most wins," Solomon rolled his eyes. "A bit of a disgrace to the knighthood if you ask me. Yet, Chalfant seemed highly respected by his current troupe. They said he was a very good fighter, despite how he used his talents."

Jax wandered further past a clump of tents, seeing a few Saphire guardsmen in front of a well-ornamented shelter. "Is that his campsite?" She motioned up ahead to the guards.

Her captain nodded. "We've been guarding it ever since Roche's men cleared out. They wouldn't let us in while they were searching. I have no idea where they found the torn cloth. Once they left, we did some investigating of our own, but found nothing useful."

Jax glided past the statuesque guards, her amethyst eyes taking a moment to adjust to the dim light of the airy chamber. She was immediately filled with surprise as she took in the expensive-looking woven tapestries and rugs adorning the tent's walls and floor. Plush chairs were positioned in a small sitting area, with just enough room for an ornately designed bed covered in silk pillows. "My, this man traveled in style. Can one really make that much money on the farcical tourney circuit?" She could not suppress her disbelief at the grandeur around her.

"When you've been at it for as long as he was, I can imagine that wealth accumulates over time." George murmured from the doorway.

"Makes you regret your decision to join the Ducal Guard, I bet?" Jax quipped in jest.

"All the fortune in the world couldn't entice me away, Your Grace," Captain Solomon said with softness, both resolute and sincere.

Blushing ever so slightly, she walked around the spacious tent, taking in the sight before her. "Did you or Roche's men put everything back in its place?"

Captain Solomon shook his head. "As far as I know, no one really touched anything."

"Interesting," Jax said as she surveyed the immaculate living space. "You'd think that there would have been evidence of a struggle or something. I mean, if the man was as good a fighter as his comrades say, you'd think there would have been a tussle of some sort. There's hardly even a stain on the floor from where he bled out." She leaned down, seeing the soiled spot on the rug, no bigger than the width of her hand.

George came to her side. "You think he was killed somewhere else?"

"Either that, or he knew the man who killed him, and was unable to fight back until it was too late," Jax surmised.

"If we know for certain that he was killed here, we might be able to vindicate Perry once we prove they were not known associates," Captain Solomon suggested.

"That won't be enough for my grandfather, unfortunately. He's out to let this destroy Saphire and Pettraud's reputations. Two birds with one stone, so they say." Jax stood, her eyes scanning the room for anything that might tell her more. "You said before that Chalfant had only recently joined the Savant knights' delegation. Do we know anything about duchies he's been to in the past?"

"I asked his companions, and they had little to offer regarding his background. One believed he was born in Hestes, while two mentioned he spent some extensive time in Tandora," Captain Solomon reported.

Looking once more at the myriad of tapestries and furnishings, Jax felt unsettled. "These pieces have come from all over the realm. He appears to be a very well-traveled man. I think I'll stop in the ducal archives here and see if I can find a record of the various places these farcical tourneys are held." Her eyes caught an elaborate golden ship's clock on a small nightstand near the bed. "It will have to wait, though, until after the hunt. I need to return to my rooms and change into my riding clothes. Keep digging into Chalfant's past, George, and do not leave this tent unattended. I want to know why this man was singled out." Taking off the shabby blanket, she did her best to wipe her face clear of dirt and grime before leaving the tent. "Come find me as soon as the hunt concludes. I'll see if I can find anything out from the knights as we ride."

With an affirmative nod, Captain Solomon retreated further into the camp on his mission. Jax watched his muscular figure disappear amongst the growing crowd, people returning to the grounds to watch the start of the hunt. Gathering her skirts, she took the quickest route through the woods she could find, fortunately not running into anyone until she crashed into her suite, startling Uma from her reading. "Your Grace! What did you do to your clothes? Your hair? Oh goodness, virtues help me." Racing to Jax's side, Uma immediately set to work on reapplying makeup and re-braiding hair, putting Jax back together from her disheveled state.

A signal horn from the courtyard warned the hunt would begin in an hour's time. "What do you think the chances are that my grandfather has reserved a horse for me?" Jax groaned, not having the time to secure her own mount that morning.

"If he did, be careful. The beast will probably buck you off its back the moment you sit down." Uma chortled, but Jax detected a note of caution in her voice, one that Jax knew she would heed.

After a few more frantic moments and many reprimands from Uma, Jax was once more in pristine condition, looking lovely as ever, ready for the hunt. "You are a miracle worker," she declared as she looked at her reflection. Giving Uma a quick kiss on the cheek, Jax slipped out of the room, making her way down to the stables. With any luck, she'd be able to find herself a solid mount.

"Jacqueline! You disappeared during breakfast, and I haven't seen you since!" Amia's singsong voice chirped down the hallway, and Jax spotted her youngest aunt near the courtyard entrance.

Uncertain of whether Duke Mensina had spread word of Perry's capture, Jax smiled tightly. "It's been a busy morning, preparing for the hunt and all. I was just on my way to the stables to find a suitable mare to ride for the event."

"Oh, you must take mine! I won't be riding this year." Amia placed a hand over her stomach. "I wouldn't want to do anything that might cause me to miscarry."

Jax's eyes widened, taking in the news. "You're with child? Congratulations, dear aunt. I know you have wanted a child of your own for the longest time." Giving her aunt an affectionate squeeze, she let herself smile with pure joy. Amia's eyes glistened with happiness as she eagerly escorted her niece to the stables. Jax let her chat away about the baby names she and her husband had discussed, but how Duke Mensina wanted their first child named after him or his late wife. Murmuring acknowledgment in all the right places, Jax kept a watchful eye on all the people they ran into as they made their way to the stables. Throngs of knights were arriving to fetch their horses, buzzing with conversation. Jax strained to eavesdrop, but Amia's prattling drowned out most of the chatter.

"Oh, that man is even more handsome in the daylight," Amia said with a longing sigh. Her sudden change in topic drew Jax's attention back to her. Following her gaze, Jax noticed her aunt staring at the backside of Sir Antoine as he brushed a brilliant white stallion with affection.

"Sir Antoine, I must say your horse is quite lovely," Amia said.

Antoine turned around and offered a pleasant response, all but ignoring Amia's blatant flirtation. "Maximus is my ultimate prize. I won him in a tournament the last time I was in Crepsta."

Jax's eyes lit up. "He's one of the Crepsta stallions? I have one back home myself: Mortimer." She took in the true beauty of the legendary breed of horses. "I don't think I've ever heard of a white Crepsta."

Antoine stroked the beast's nose fondly. "He's one of a kind. That's why he was the ultimate prize. He's quite special. Been with me for years." The knight's focus drifted to Jax as he took in her riding outfit. "I see you are joining us for the hunt, Your Grace. It will be an honor to have you amongst the ranks. Surely, the stags will come right up to you once they see your beauty."

Jax rolled her eyes, while Amia giggled girlishly at the man's flirtation. "Perhaps you will join my niece at the head of the column?" she suggested in a coquettish manner. "You can keep her entertained so that my father doesn't bore her to death." Amia nudged Jax closer to the famed knight.

Jax's eyes narrowed in retort, but Antoine beat her to a response. "While I would love to be by the Duchess's side, I believe that is Lord Pettraud's rightful place."

At the mention of Perry, Jax's heart turned heavy. Once the hunt concluded, she would see if she could sneak down to his holding cell to visit him. She knew he was counting on her to clear his name, and he'd want to know all they had found out.

"I don't think Lord Pettraud will be making the hunt," Amia said. "My father mentioned that the poor thing was not feeling well after last night's festivities and has taken to his rooms for the day," Amia explained, clearly intent on her niece befriending the Knight with No Face. Her aunt's statement also told Jax that Duke Mensina was keeping Perry's imprisonment quiet for now.

"Well, Lady Amia, here you and I are gabbing away about what should suit the Duchess, and we haven't even asked her." Sir Antoine turned his dark amber eyes back to Jax, their intensity making her knees shake uncharacteristically.

"Of course, you should accompany me up front, Sir Antoine. Who knows, perhaps the deer will prefer your golden hair to mine," Jax gushed superficially, wanting this conversation to end. "But excuse me for now. I must get myself a horse. I left Mortimer back in Saphire."

"Oh, silly me, I forgot that's why we came down here." Amia

chuckled absentmindedly. "Well, good day, Sir Antoine. I hope your arrows fly fast and true." With that, she dragged Jax away into the stables and introduced her to a svelte chestnut bay mare with an endearing temperament. "Her name is Olive."

Within the next ten minutes, the stable hands saddled Olive, giving Jax just enough time to canter over to the hunt's starting line. Despite her initial unease with riding a strange horse, the Duchess's heart quickly softened for the beautiful animal. Olive was mild and sweet, unfazed by the commotion around her, as Jax urged her through the ranks of knights, joining Duke Mensina at the front of the pack.

"Glad you could join us, Jacqueline." Her grandfather grumbled, not sounding pleased at all.

"I wouldn't miss it, Grand-Père," Jax countered, grabbing the leather braided reigns firmly in her hand to keep steady. For a ducal hunt, women riding with the column always had to sit side-saddle, which was the absolute worst, causing Jax to endlessly shift in her seat. She'd only been mounted for five minutes or so and already wanted to give up and get off, but seeing her grandfather's brooding expression, she knew she was in it for the long haul.

A small page boy appeared off to the side, a golden bugle in hand. Seeing the signal from the Duke, the little boy puffed his cheeks, sounding the start of the hunt. Horses hastened forward instinctively at the call, hounds barking beneath their powerful legs. Jax felt Olive lurch forward, and they were off.

Chapter Seven

Mesmerized by the creature's beauty, Jax watched Maximus gather speed until the horse galloped beside her, Sir Antoine grinning boyishly in her direction. She knew the thrill of riding a Crepsta stallion at top speed, and it was nearly impossible not to smile. "He rides beautifully, Sir Antoine," Jax complimented as she watched the beast thunder across the ground.

"You're very good in the saddle, yourself, Duchess," Antoine commented, noting her exquisite posture as he slowed down to trot beside her.

She laughed. "I wish my High Courtier could hear you say that. I was always a fan of riding with both feet in the stirrups as a child. He practically had to tie me to a saddle like this to get me to sit like a lady," she shared, groaning at the hours Jaquobie spent ranting and raving about her inadequate equestrian skills.

"I can imagine you were quite the wild spirit as a child." Antoine smiled, chuckling at the thought. "You are quite refreshing from the other ducal rulers I've dealt with in the past."

Jax frowned slightly, hoping he was not implying that she was weaker than her male or more experienced counterparts in the realm.

He saw her expression and immediately backtracked. "What I meant to convey was that your open-mind and kind attitude is uplifting. I'm so used to listening to dukes drone on and on about themselves," he added, rolling his eyes, then blushed, realizing that Duke Mensina was only a few feet away. "You seem to be genuinely interested in others around you. It's nice."

For the first time since they were introduced, Jax felt a rush of fondness for the knight. His elaborate and gaudy persona was just an act, a way to keep the mystery alive, now that he was no longer nameless. From atop his stately horse, Antoine revealed his true colors and what he valued. "Thank you, Sir Antoine. That's very kind of you."

"Wincaester! Take lead of the right column and I'll go off to the left. We'll corner the little devils in no time," Duke Mensina's harsh command interrupted their intimate conversation, causing Antoine to spring into action.

Having no desire to stay with her grandfather, Jax nudged Olive after the group Antoine led deeper into the forest. She had fallen behind, now that the chase was on, and she dallied at the back of the column with a few bannermen. Men she noticed wearing the colors of Savant.

Seizing the opportunity to learn more about the fallen knight, she edged her horse closer to the group. "I'm so sorry to hear about the death of Master Chalfant." Jax said with sympathy, addressing the man nearest to her.

He did a double take, likely thrown by her being the Duchess of Saphire, and yet still speaking to them. "Excuse me, Your Grace? What did you say?"

Jax leaned in as much as the saddle would allow. "I said I'm sorry to hear about Master Chalfant's death."

The man looked at his other comrades, each of whom appeared spooked.

"Forgive me, did I say something offensive?" Jax couldn't understand their odd behavior.

One of the other young men spoke up. "No, ma'am. We were just surprised you knew about his passing, that's all. We were under orders from the Duke not to mention it during the festival."

Jax's brows rose. "He ordered you to keep it a secret?"

Another nodded eagerly. "Yes, Your Grace. He gave us each ten gold pieces and promised us ten more at the festival's end if we kept our word."

"Duke Mensina paid you?" Jax's mouth fell fully agape. She knew her grandfather could be ruthless, but she didn't think he would stoop quite so low to keep this a secret.

"Yeah, miss. We imagine it would be quite the blemish on the feast if a man died from having too much fun," squeaked the youngest, likely a page boy.

Interesting. Jax's eyes washed over the entire group. So, these young men seemed totally unaware that their companion had been purposefully murdered.

"We've kept our mouths shut, but it's so hard with all the guards asking us questions about him. I mean, we didn't even know him that well, so there's not much to tell. Got no family to notify, either." The oldest appealed to Jax, likely hoping she wouldn't blow the whistle on them.

"Yes, it sounds quite tragic." Jax murmured in agreement.

"We don't know nothing about his personal life. Mostly kept to himself." One of the bannermen shrugged. "I couldn't believe it when I heard some wench had been asking after him today, hinting that she was pregnant with his baby. Poor thing is in for a rude awakening."

Jax balked, realizing they were talking about her disguise.

Trying to keep her face neutral, she pushed further for information. "Why were you surprised that he had a lady friend?"

"Didn't seem to be the type to fall for a woman like that, Your Grace. Like I said, he mostly kept to himself." The young man scratched his head. "He struck me as a bit paranoid, always thinking someone was after his money. I doubt he'd let a random woman into his tent for fear she'd rob him blind."

Jax processed this new information. Chalfant must have known his murderer if he trusted them enough to allow them entry into his tent.

"Duchess!" Sir Antoine's call startled her, forcing her to grip Olive's mane tightly to prevent herself from tumbling to the ground. Looking over her shoulder, she saw the dashing knight trotting toward her, his expression dismayed. "I guess I'm not much of a hunter after spending my life in the arena. I'm afraid we've lost the trail on this side. Hopefully, the Duke's men will track them down, so we won't all starve." He joked, nodding in acknowledgment to the ragged group of men she was speaking to. "I'll escort you back to the palace, if you'd like?" He cast a wary eye on her present company.

"Yes, that would be wonderful." She breathed a sigh of relief, thankful that the hunt hadn't lasted very long. Men were so quick to overlook animal survival instincts, and she always doubted the success of large, hollering groups in these scenarios. To her unwitting informants she said, "Thank you so much for your conversation. Again, my sympathies."

"Quite the odd company to keep, Duchess." Antoine commented dryly on their way back to the castle.

"You sound like my grandfather," Jax retorted, defending the honor of the young men.

Flushing with embarrassment, the dashing knight conceded. "I suppose you're right. I was just praising your virtues, and now I go and poke fun at you for it."

"And still, I persist." Jax smiled confidently, although the truth of it burned in her chest. She was a new breed of sovereign, trying to usher in an era of fairness and well-being for her people and the realm. She longed for the day when there was a changing of the guard and the old ducal sovereigns stepped down, leaving the world to the next generation.

"What are you thinking about?" Antoine's voice sounded gentle and curious.

"About a day when kindness is the norm of the realm, a day when people are not surprised their ruler actually takes an interest in their everyday lives," the Duchess mused, taking in the regal palace growing before them in the distance.

The Knight with No Face whistled longingly. "What a day that will be, indeed."

Chapter Eight

By the time Jax and Antoine arrived back at the palace, she felt that she had found a kindred spirit, and her heart was filled with warmth and cheerfulness. She'd learned quite a bit about his background as they trotted along. Hailing from a prominent noble family in Beautraud, Antoine Wincaester had not been fond of the spotlight shining on him from an early age. At twelve, he begged his parents to send him to live with relatives in Hestes, and there he grew into his own, realizing he could use his status in life for the good of others. Under the guise of the Knight with No Face, he could amass his own private wealth, which he used to fund schools in poor communities and clinics in towns without a resident physician. Listening to his philanthropic accomplishments, it amazed Jax that he did it all anonymously, considering his showy personality.

"I used to be afraid that if everyone found out that playboy Antoine was the secret benefactor to so many people, they would think I was after something in return. As the Knight with No Face, I could do all these things without my motivations being scrutinized.

It sounds silly now, which is why I decided to give up the double life. Now, I'm hoping to rebrand myself so that I can continue doing the work the Knight with No Face started," Antoine explained as he helped her off Olive, Jax's legs having fallen asleep from being pinched by the saddle.

"Rebrand yourself? How so?" Jax asked curiously.

"Well, the playboy image is getting a bit tiresome to uphold. I mean," he sighed dramatically at her bemusement, "a man can only handle so many women."

She poked his arm with her elbow as she rolled her eyes laboriously. "You're ridiculous."

Antoine feigned an injury, tenderly rubbing his arm. "In all seriousness, I want to settle down. I've met many beautiful women in my life, but I want someone with whom I can share my innermost thoughts with and converse about things other than the latest fashions or which Duke is hiding his mistress in a bunker."

Jax stared into his eyes, a sad loneliness building behind the deep amber. "A bunker? Really?"

Antoine blinked for a moment, the tension between them dissolving. "Some men don't treasure women the way they should, that's for sure." He cleared his throat, his attention turning to the castle. "Lord Pettraud seems like a fine man. An extremely lucky one, at the very least. I should let you get back to him, Duchess. It's been a pleasure." With a fluid bow, the Knight with No Face disappeared into the crowd leading up to the castle for the evening's festivities.

Jax felt a tinge of disappointment that her future consort had already been selected, a dark thought which immediately gave way to a rush of shame. For all his charms, Jax did not agree with Antoine's decision to create the Knight with No Face persona; she felt that a person who had the power to do good, should. It was as simple as that. She thought his reasons for hiding his philanthropy were more selfish than anything. Perry, on the other hand, had always demonstrated his inherent goodness and never felt the need to hide his true self from the world, regardless of the pain and punishment it brought from his gruff father. Thinking about the stark differences in the character of the two men, Jax chided herself for dallying behind. She wanted to visit Perry to make sure he was managing all right, as well as stop by the ducal archives to see if Mensina housed any record of the tourney schedules throughout the realm.

She veered left as she wove her way through the gardens, knowing the most direct way to the dungeons was through the sprawling kitchens. The rumbling in her stomach coaxed her to move quickly, and she realized that she had forgotten to eat lunch due to the earlier chaos. The aroma of venison stew wafted toward her, momentarily diverting her focus. She followed the scent into the heart of the kitchens, navigating skillfully out of sight of the palace staff. Her keen eyes noticed a trolley being loaded with heaping platters of fruits, pastries, cheeses, and vegetables. Nimbly, her fingers swiped a gooey cherry strudel, stuffing it rudely into her mouth. She felt the sugar seep into her bloodstream, giving her the second wind she needed.

Following a winding hall away from the kitchens, the cool air signaled her descent into the depths of the castle. As a child, she had been forbidden from going into the dark recesses of the palace, so naturally she took every chance she could get to sneak down. At least until a toothless prisoner scared the wits out of her, the memory still very much ingrained in her psyche.

"Pardon me, Your Grace, may I assist you?" Reginald's slimy voice startled her from a dark corner. Despite his polite words, the Master Steward's tone suggested he was in no mood to help.

Calming her pounding heart, she delivered a cool stare. "Why, yes, I wanted to check on Lord Pettraud to ensure his safety and well-being. The Duke of Pettraud will obviously expect a full report about his son's unjustified imprisonment." Seeing the steward's eye narrow, she knew she had touched a nerve.

"I understand your concern, Duchess, but we do not allow visitors." Reginald's words were sharp and pointed.

"I believe it is the right of a sovereign to visit her subject, should they be detained," Jax snapped with fury, throwing her shoulders back in defiance.

"That is true, Your Grace. But unfortunately, in this situation, Lord Pettraud is not officially a citizen of Saphire," Reginald countered, sleazy triumph dripping from his eyes.

Jax opened her mouth to protest but then closed it, realizing Perry would not legally be tied to Saphire until they married. Clenching her fists, she struggled to give the steward a conciliatory smile. "I shall speak to my grandfather about this matter. Good day, Steward." Not bothering to wait for his reply, she turned on her heel and marched out of the dank darkness back toward her apartment chambers, fuming at the man's snide comments. She was so outraged that not until she arrived at the door to her suite did she remember that she meant to visit the ducal archives.

Unlike Saphire, which also boasted a huge library in the capital city of Sephretta, Mensina's only archives were situated in northern tower of the palace. With a calculating glance at the dial on the wall, Jax cursed, realizing she had very little time until she was expected back at the banquet hall for the second night of the feast. Barging into her quarters, she began loosening the laces of her corset so she could wriggle out of it without assistance. "Uma!" Jax called into her maid's room, adjacent to her apartment. "Dear one, I need you to do something very important."

"I doubt fixing your hair qualifies as something of importance," Uma said dryly as she popped her head into the room. Seeing Jax's exasperated expression, her teasing grin left her face. "What's wrong?"

"I know I promised you could attend the feast each night, but I need you to do something for me. I would do it myself but my absence would raise too many suspicions." Jax filled her in on Perry's imprisonment and what she had learned so far about Master Chalfant. "I need you to go to the ducal archives and track down for me the different places these farcical tourneys have been held over the past ten years or so. Find, if you can, the dates and the hosting cities of each event. That might help prove Perry's innocence."

Uma's shoulders straightened in pride, obviously touched that Jax trusted her enough to request her assistance on this mission. "Of course, I'll go there right away if you don't need my help getting ready." Her eyes widened as she awaited Jax's response to the unspoken question.

Jax waved a hand, shooing her away with playful reproach. "I am perfectly capable, although my makeup won't look nearly as flawless as it does when applied by your hand."

Ducking out of the room, Uma disappeared on her quest, leaving Jax to prepare herself for the rapidly approaching dinner party. Tonight was meant to be a much more intimate affair, with her grandfather hosting only the courtiers traveling with their duchy's delegation. The thought of being surrounded by stuffy men who would be analyzing and appraising her every move caused a groan of agitation to float out of her lips. If only Perry could be by her side, it would make the gathering more bearable. She wished more than anything that she could sneak down to the fairgrounds and eat with the knights, who were no doubt celebrating the completion of the hunt.

Just as she placed her selected crown jewels on her loose, flowing hair, a knock on her door startled her. "Jax, are you still in there?" George Solomon's voice whispered from the other side of the dense wood.

Unlocking the door, she ushered him inside. "Well, have you found anything of use? They won't allow me to see Perry, George.

I'm getting worried that my grandfather is going to harm him out of spite."

Captain Solomon ran a hand through his hair, his face troubled. "I wish I had better news to report. I thought that perhaps money motivated this, but apparently Chalfant recently settled all his debts with his last stint in Savant. He was a man with no known enemies."

Jax stomped her foot in frustration, the heel of her golden slipper digging painfully into her skin as a result. "We're right back to where we started. Hopefully Uma has more luck. I've asked her to track down the farcical tourney locations and see if we can clear Perry's name that way. The Mensina tournament was the first time his father let him travel outside the duchy, so if we can prove their paths could not have crossed before now, then there's hardly motive for Perry to commit such a deed."

"I agree, your logic makes sense, Jax, but I'm beginning to think no matter what we do, your grandfather will find a way to thwart us. We had to relinquish guarding Chalfant's tent because Roche and his men ordered us out. I couldn't stay without causing a scene." George looked quite defeated. It didn't suit his handsome face well.

"At least we have several eyewitnesses in our own Ducal Guard who can attest to the state of the tent." Jax grumbled, pacing around the room.

"You think Duke Mensina's men would plant evidence or something?" Captain Solomon seemed shocked by the accusation.

Jax gave him a cool look. "I wouldn't put anything past my grandfather if it meant undermining me or Saphire." She sighed, looking out the window. "We never should have come to this place." Looking at the time, she rolled her eyes. "I must get going, George. I'll find you later once I've spoken with Uma."

Her captain bowed and shuffled aside as she took off for the dining room, trying to rearrange her scowl into something that passed for a meager smile. It was only when she saw Sir Antoine

Wincaester's figure strolling ahead of her did her expression feel genuine. "Antoine? Are you joining us for dinner this evening?"

Hearing her melodic voice, he turned with a deep bow. "Unfortunately for you, I did not make the cut. Luckily for me, I get to head down to the fairgrounds and spend some time getting to properly know my comrades. I feel like I've been cooped up in this palace for too long."

Jax's disappointment in his absence was sincere. "What a shame. It would have been nice to have someone to talk to." She fiddled absently with the ruffles of her gown.

Antoine gave her a curious look. "Is Lord Pettraud not accompanying you this evening?"

Reddening at the slip of her tongue, Jax shuffled her feet awkwardly. "Something he ate this morning didn't agree with him, so he's indisposed tonight," she lied with ease. To her relief, Antoine nodded his head in acceptance.

"Well, do pass on my wishes to him for a speedy recovery." With a farewell bow, the Knight with No Face departed for the castle doors, leaving Jax to face the evening alone.

‡

As hard as she tried to suppress them, yawns assaulted her throughout the dull dinner party. If it weren't for the luscious-looking bumbleberry cake sitting primly on display, waiting to be served for dessert, she would have claimed a headache and left halfway through the first course. The sweet, fluffy frosting was worth a night of suffering, and by ten o'clock, she was strolling back to her room in gluttonous pain, her stomach feeling like it was going to burst through the seams of her ocean blue dress.

Uma greeted her in the suite's sitting room, wringing her hands anxiously as her Duchess strolled in.

Jax hurried to the woman's side. "Have you found anything of note, dear one?"

Uma's chestnut brown eyes crinkled with worried anticipation. "I did manage to come across a planner chronicling all the different tourneys in the realm. These farcical tournaments regularly pop up in Hestes, Crepsta, Tandora, Beautraud, Isla DeLacqua, and," she paused, her face paling at the implication, "Pettraud."

The cake flipped in Jax's stomach, a wave of nausea flooding in. "No! Virtue's sake, this makes matters worse for Perry. If my grandfather learns of this connection, he'll use it against us."

"No one was in the archives with me except the curator, and I told him I wanted to view the records because my long-lost brother was rumored to be roaming the lands as a jester." Uma hurried to Jax's side in confidence.

Jax gave her maid a grateful smile, silently praising her for her ingenuity. "Let's hope no one finds out while we are here that you have no siblings." Squeezing Uma's hand with affection, Jax suddenly felt overwhelmingly tired. She was no closer to clearing Perry's name than when she'd begun this fruitless investigation. "Thank you, Uma. You did well. Share what you've learned with Captain Solomon. He'll want to know. I'd go myself, but I feel a bit out of sorts. Perhaps a good night's sleep will help me figure things out. I must have missed something." She lost herself in thought as Uma prepared her for bed, her mind spinning as she lay her head against the fluffed bed pillows.

She didn't realize she'd fallen off to sleep until a firm hand gently shook her shoulder, coaxing her awake. "Jax! Jax, I need you to wake up now."

Her eyes foggy with lingering dreams, she squinted, staring up at the Captain of the Ducal Guard. "George? Virtue's sake, what time is it? What's going on?" She sat up, cognition slowly returning to her confused gaze.

Captain Solomon knelt at her bedside, his brow furrowed. "I need you to come with me, Duchess. There's been an incident and I need your help."

His apprehensive tone launched her out of bed without asking any further questions. Grabbing a robe to cover her nightgown, she threw a traveling cloak over her shoulders, tucking her unkempt hair into the hood. "Lead the way, Captain."

He cautioned silence as they stole through the maze of hallways, unable to answer the barrage of questions pummeling through her mind. It was only when the castle air grew cooler that she realized he was leading her into the belly of the palace. This route was unfamiliar to her, so she guessed they were not heading towards the dungeons. She'd been hoping her captain had managed to get her an audience with Perry, but the smells of decay and incense triggered her recognition. They were heading for the catacombs.

Just as she was about to turn a corner, Captain Solomon held out his arm and halted her, his keen eyes scanning the darkness for activity. Pulling her into the shadows of a doorway, he reached for an iron doorknob. "Forgive all the secrecy, Jax, but we only have a few moments before the physician returns to prepare the body."

"Body?" Jax's shock echoed around them, and she immediately cursed her indiscretion. "What is going on, George?" she whispered, suddenly queasy of what lay on the other side of the door.

"There's been another death. A young woman's body was found in the woods just north of the fairgrounds," Captain Solomon somberly reported.

Jax shivered, knowing she'd walked through those woods merely hours before. "Was she attacked by an animal?" she asked in hopeful naiveté.

Stony-faced, George replied, "I'm afraid not. From what my men and I have gathered, she was strangled. I wanted to see the body for myself."

"Was it really necessary to bring me?" Jax asked, her skin tingling with goosebumps.

"Yes, I think you'll see why in just a moment. Prepare yourself, Duchess. This will be unpleasant." The captain noiselessly pushed open the door to the preparation chamber, a hallowed cavern smelling of perfumed flesh and blood.

Suppressing a gag, Jax followed her captain, her eyes immediately narrowing in on a covered figure lying on a slab in the center of the room. The sight felt like déjà vu, the vision of her father's body blossoming morbidly in her mind. "Tell me why I'm here, Captain," she demanded, holding her breath at the stench.

Pulling back the stained sheet, George Solomon revealed the victim to the flickering torchlight. In the uneven darkness, Jax could tell the woman was of slender build, no more than twenty years of age, but with the weathered skin of a hard life making her appear older and more mature. Her blond hair was streaked with dirt, darkening its shade, and in the stoicness of death, it looked as though the woman had been very pretty. "The poor girl."

The captain nodded in agreement. From the corner of her eye, Jax could have sworn George's face paled uncharacteristically as he assessed the body. While the woman's death was tragic, the captain's intense reaction surprised her. "What's wrong?"

Captain Solomon's brows raised in incredulity. "Does she remind you of anyone?"

Frowning in concentration, Jax looked back at the woman's face, trying to figure out what George was hinting at. The woman was quite beautiful with her high cheeks, full lips, and dark, honey colored hair…

"She looks like me." The disturbing realization crushed the breath from Jax's lungs. Staggering back, she clasped a hand to her dry throat. "What have I done?" She thought back to her adventure down to the fairgrounds, disguising herself as a tourney wench, alluding to the galley master that she was pregnant with the dead man's baby. Tears obscured her vision and guilt ripped through her chest. Someone had come after this woman because they thought she was Chalfant's mistress. This woman was dead because of a story she had made up on a whim. "The murderer thought she was with Chalfant's child," Jax croaked, looking to her captain for forgiveness. "She was killed because of me."

Captain Solomon replaced the sheet reverently, taking a few moments to gather his thoughts. "We're dealing with a dangerous man here, Jax. This woman was killed because of her suspected connections to Chalfant."

Feeling dizzy, Jax backed further away from the morbid table, leaning on the cool stone wall for support. "What is it about this Chalfant character that we're missing? To kill him is one thing, but to murder a woman solely because she knew him intimately is another."

George came to her side and guided her into the hallway, away from the guilt and blame plaguing her. "You told me that the Savant delegation said Chalfant mostly kept to himself and that they were incredulous to hear the rumor he'd befriended a tourney wench," he recounted.

Eager to preoccupy her mind with a puzzle, Jax followed along. "Yes, and it seems our killer heard the same rumor." She gazed down the dark corridors leading back to her apartment. "Maybe he was afraid that Chalfant had found a confidant and shared something."

"Something worth killing her for?" George mused. "Like what?"

Jax shrugged dejectedly, but felt she might be on to something. "Chalfant was obviously killed for a reason. And if our killer thought someone else might be privy to that reason, what would stop him from killing again to protect it?"

"But how does framing Lord Pettraud fit into all of this?" Captain Solomon asked, pointing out a large gap in their understanding of events.

"Well, it really doesn't at this moment. Besides, Perry was only framed for Chalfant's murder. The young woman was an afterthought." Jax cringed, shame and regret clawing at her. "Her murder was a loose end the killer had to tie up after he heard the rumors generated by my appearance at the fairgrounds."

"Do you think your grandfather will believe these two deaths are connected, and committed by the same person?" George's heavy tone told her what he believed to be the answer.

"My grandfather has had it out for Perry this entire time, so I don't expect him to listen to our theory, especially since we don't have a suspect of our own." Jax scowled as she folded her arms. "I wouldn't be surprised if he was somehow orchestrating this whole thing himself."

The captain let out a low whistle. "You think he'd stoop to murder?"

"That's how he wanted my mother to deal with my father, did you know that? I doubt he's mellowed in his old age." Guessing from the shock in George's eyes, Duke Mensina's assassination plot came as news to him.

By now, they had arrived at her suite and paused at the door. "We should consider any connections Duke Mensina may have had to Chalfant," Jax said. "Perhaps the man did something to affront my grandfather and he took it as an opportunity to kill two birds with one stone."

"I'll have my men look into it in the morning. Meanwhile, I want you to stay out of this for now, Jax. It's not safe for you or for the duchy if you get caught stirring the pot with your grandfather." Captain Solomon gave her a pointed look. She knew he was fighting the urge to mention that her thoughtless meddling had resulted in the death of an innocent young woman.

"I want you to report back to me on your findings no later than lunchtime, Captain," Jax commanded without acknowledging his statement before closing her door for the night.

Chapter Nine

A knock at the door pulled Jax from her late-morning reverie. She was relieved to see Captain Solomon poke his head into the room. Her hopes quickly deflated when she saw his dour expression. "No news, I take it?" She motioned for him to take the chair next to her.

Shaking his head, he sat down in defeat. "Word amongst Roche's men is that the woman's death is entirely unrelated to Chalfant's, considering Chalfant's killer is already imprisoned."

Jax's blood boiled at the preposterous belief of Perry being a murderer. "I'll speak with my grandfather this afternoon and present our case to him."

At this, the captain's head whipped up, his eyes dark with warning. "No. It is too dangerous for you, Duchess. Considering the possibility that Duke Mensina might be in on the whole thing, I want you to keep him at an arm's distance."

Jax snorted, her disgust quite unladylike. "That's going to be hard with the ball this evening. I'm supposed to sit next to him at the ducal table."

Captain Solomon rolled his eyes, as if he were dealing with a child. "You know what I meant. I don't want you facing off with him until we have a better understanding of what's going on and whether or not your safety is at risk."

Not one to take a reprimand sitting down, Jax stood from her own plush chair. "Then I suggest you figure this whole debacle out." With a dismissive strut, she fled her apartment, needing a moment to collect her thoughts. Wandering idly down the hallway, she came to Perry's abandoned suite, which she remembered the moment she laid eyes on it, was not vacant. Hendrie was to have taken up residence to keep a watchful eye on things. Knocking on the door, she rearranged her face to a regal expression just as the young man opened the door, surprise in his eyes at having a visitor.

"Your Grace! I was just on my way to see you. I may have found something that might prove of interest to you." Hendrie's eyes were wide with excitement as he ushered her inside the large room.

Jax sat down, drumming her fingers on her thigh as the valet retreated into the bedroom. He vanished only a moment before he returned with something in the palm of his hand. "I found this in Lord Pettraud's closet. It must have fallen into one of his slippers. I only came across it because I was polishing his dress shoes." Holding out a trembling hand in anticipation, Hendrie presented Jax with his find.

At first glance, it looked like a bronze medallion, the award of a contest or some such thing. Jax picked it up, turning the small piece over, spying a large, lavish X engraved in the precious metal. The other side simply boasted a name, "LeDuke," etched in scrawling writing. What was this, some type of crest? "Have you any idea what this is, Hendrie?"

Looking dejected, the valet shook his head. "None, my lady. I thought you might know. Perhaps it's a symbol of a noble house?"

"This does not belong to any noble house I know of," Jax

murmured, more to herself than to him. She wracked her brain, visions of the realm's extensive family trees flooding her well-trained mind.

The door to Perry's apartment opened behind them, and a chastened-looking Captain Solomon appeared. Whatever words he planned to say died in his mouth when his keen eyes narrowed in on the object in Jax's hand. "Where did you find that?" His curiosity was mixed with hesitance.

Hendrie explained once more how he had stumbled across the bronze piece in Perry's closet. "You've seen this before, haven't you, George?" Jax coaxed, seeing the flash of recognition in the guardsman's suspicious eyes.

"Yes, I have, although how it came to be in Lord Pettraud's rooms, I have no idea." Captain Solomon plucked the medallion from Jax's hand, holding it up to reflect in the streaming sunlight. "This is known as a Shadow Seal. It's the official crest of the Shadow Brethren."

"Shadow Brethren?" Jax repeated. "I thought they were a myth."

"In Saphire, they are. Your father ran them out a long time ago. However, other duchies have not been as successful. The Shadow Brethren's power has been festering for years. In the beginning, it was merely a guild for thieves and bandits, but as their power and influence grew, so did the scope of their crimes. Nowadays, the best assassins are protected by the Brethren." Captain Solomon's teeth gritted as he clenched the seal. "This is very troubling."

"This is the proof we needed!" Jax leaped to her feet, feeling victorious. "Perry is being framed by these rogues."

The captain's face darkened. "The Shadow Brethren are hired help, Jax. Someone else is likely footing the bill while they do the dirty work."

The Duchess felt her face go white. "I wouldn't put it past my grandfather. That might explain why he demanded I attend this ridiculous feast in the first place. Perhaps this has all been an elaborate setup to take Saphire down."

Hendrie whimpered at the accusation, Captain Solomon's harsh look silencing the young man. "If we can prove the Duke is financing the Brethren, we may have a chance at catching him." The weary man wandered around the room. "We need to speak to the ducal camerlengo. Perhaps one of us can charm their way into getting the information we need?" He cocked a suggestive eyebrow at Jax.

Her eyes sparkled at the hint. "Of course. But my grandfather could have covered up the transactions very easily, or possibly used his own private reserves for payment," she pointed out, well-versed in the numerous ways Dukes could launder money without anyone being the wiser. It was one of the first lessons her father taught her. Not every leader had their people's best interests at heart.

"We have to start somewhere." Captain Solomon thanked Hendrie for his diligence and escorted Jax back to her room, their tiff already forgotten.

"It will have to wait until tomorrow morning, I'm afraid. If I'm not present for the ball, it will surely raise questions that we don't want to be asked." Jax cast an anxious look at the clock. "Poor Perry. I can't believe I've gotten him tangled up in this mess."

"Perhaps I can do some research this evening while everyone else is at the ball. I'm sure I'll be able to finesse my way into the treasury room," George reassured her, taking his leave to allow her enough time to get ready. It took all her restraint to keep from trailing after him, but she needed to be mindful that her duchy's reputation was at stake. Tonight's ball was rumored to be the most elaborate event Duke Mensina had thrown in years, and several sovereigns were said to be joining the Feast of Champions for the evening.

"Shall we begin, Jax?" Uma waved a powder-covered brush, motioning to the seat in front of the vanity mirror.

"Do your worst," the Duchess jested as her lady's maid set to work on her transformation.

Chapter Ten

"My, Jacqueline, I don't think I've ever seen such a beautiful sight before in my life," Annette complimented as her niece entered the small royal chamber attached to the ballroom.

Her other aunts tittered their agreement. Jax felt her face coloring at the unwanted attention. Her ball gown billowed to the floor, the lavender silk shining in the candlelight. Her caramel hair was woven skillfully into a regal crest, her most dazzling gold crown resting securely, the blue and green gems radiating her power. Uma had used more makeup than she normally did to complete the dramatic look, to the point that Jax hardly recognized herself in the mirror.

Her family gathered together as they waited for the courtiers to announce their official arrival. Duke Mensina was noticeably absent from the group, causing Jax's mind to spin with wild conclusions. She couldn't imagine what could be keeping her grandfather from his hosting duties at the most important party of the year, but she had suspicions that she desperately wished weren't true. *If he is indeed tangled up in this mess, I'm sure he has more pressing matters on his mind.*

Jax watched her aunts chatter on as if nothing were amiss. It nearly broke her heart that she'd been so quick to pin these murders on her grandfather, but after years of strained silence and feuding, should she really expect anything else? She remembered listening to the courtiers who'd been sent to extend the invitation to attend the Feast of Champions, part of her praying to the virtues that her grandfather finally wanted a clean slate. They'd lost so much because of the tension; perhaps it was time to bury the hatchet. Her hopes had quickly been dashed, as her grandfather's request came across as more of a command than genuine invitation.

As their wait grew longer and the crowd in the ballroom became audibly restless, Annette took charge, her forehead wrinkled in concern. "I suppose I shall take over as hostess, since Father appears to be detained." She instructed her sisters to assemble tightly behind her and gave Jax an apologetic smile. "You'll enter after us, Jacqueline."

This suited the Duchess fine, as there was no doubt the guests would gossip about Duke Mensina's absence, paying no attention to her when she entered. She was here merely to show her ability to carry on quite well without her father's guidance, nothing more. She would do her due diligence and mingle with the visiting Dukes and Duchesses, but she could refrain from talk of political alliances and networking, given her duchy's position in the Realm of Virtues.

She was right in her prediction that Duke Mensina's failure to attend his own ball catapulted the room into a frenzy of speculation, allowing her to slip in almost completely unnoticed. For a while, she watched her aunts try to remain calm in the face of the sudden turmoil, giving reassurances to their more important guests that their host for the evening would be with them shortly. Few of the visiting Dukes even bothered to approach her, and none of the Duchesses even looked her way. Their sour expressions told her they were displeased with her successful reign thus far.

"How is it that the most beautiful woman in the room is standing here all alone?" A familiar voice pulled her out of her thoughts, forcing her to furtively pop the rest of a half-eaten fudge bonbon in her mouth. Sir Antoine laughed as he watched her devour the treat.

Refusing to be embarrassed by her love of sugar, Jax wiped her lips free of chocolate. "Perhaps everyone senses my reluctance. Dances were never a favorite of mine, even growing up. Too little opportunity to eat." She motioned to the small plate of food resting on a high-topped table next to her. "The size of this plate is pitiful. I had no room for vegetables."

Boldly, Antoine reached out a nimble finger and plucked a chocolate-covered strawberry from her stash. "I agree that this is all a bit tedious. Give me a joust followed by a raucous feast, any day."

Scowling at the empty spot on her tiny platter, Jax surveyed the man with renewed interest. "Why are you really giving up your life as the Knight with No Face? I'm sorry, but I find it hard to believe your philanthropy is the reason."

Antoine stroked the stubble sprouting from his chin. "I guess I was getting tired of it all. Probably rather impulsive on my part. I decided the day I set out from Beautraud to attend the feast that this would be my final hurrah. I sent one of my men ahead of our party to let Duke Mensina know I would be making my announcement at the festival. It's only a shame I didn't take home one last win in the contest against Lord Pettraud."

Jax thought back to that day and how pleased the Duke had been that the Knight with No Face had chosen to announce his retirement in the Mensina dukedom. "Well, I'm sure your legacy overshadows that one defeat."

Antoine chuckled, looking around at the splendor as he caught his breath. "Yes, I can only hope. And even if I've been disgraced by it, I'll just take my winnings from the tournament and hide away back in Beautraud."

It took Jax a moment to realize that he referred to the prize money from the Tournament of Virtues they were all gathered here to celebrate. "I imagine some of the knights were displeased by the fact my grandfather withheld their winnings for so long."

Antoine shrugged. "He explained it well enough. He wanted to truly celebrate our achievements after he had time to mourn his daughter's death." The former Knight with No Face suddenly looked abashed, as if just realizing he'd been speaking about Jax's mother. "Although from what I've heard across the fairgrounds, everyone was quite surprised that we received the invite so soon."

To one not of ducal blood, she imagined it would seem rather crass to host such a lavish event so soon after a beloved daughter's demise, but emotions in the royal world tended to be caged and concealed. Not wanting to dwell on the uncomfortable topic, Jax longingly gazed at the doorway. "What would you say to a walk in the gardens? It's a lovely evening out. We can nab some more strawberries, too." She motioned her head toward a platter floating by on the shoulder of a servant, scooping up three more treats to add to her heaping plate.

Antoine reached for some of his own and followed obediently behind her as they made their escape from the swarming ballroom. A light summer breeze cooled her bare shoulders as she waltzed into the moonlight, winding her way to a bench by a flickering torch. "Now, this is much more my style." She giggled devilishly, popping another chocolate-dipped fruit into her watering mouth.

They ate in companionable silence, the humming of elegant violins and cellos dancing on the soft wind from the grand ball. "This is much better, Duchess. Brilliant idea," Antoine said as he reached for another piece of chocolate, shuffling closer to her.

"Ouch!" she squealed, something sharp poking into her side. She felt her face flush red with embarrassment, disliking how girlishly flippant she sounded.

"Goodness me! My sincere apologies. Sometimes I forget this isn't a toy." Antoine fumbled at his belt, pulling forward an incredible, uniquely hilted dagger. The torch flames sparkling overhead reflected on the weapon. Jax reached out a finger to stroke the spiraled handle, nearly as long as the sheathed blade, thinking how familiar it looked, a fuzzy memory from her childhood floating just out of sight.

"Is this a unicorn horn?" she gasped in wonder, the pearly grip suddenly sparking a vision in her mind.

Antoine grinned, impressed. "Indeed. I won it off a Cetachi merchant a long time ago. It's gotten me out of many a predicament in the past. Sometimes, the hilt is more dangerous than the actual silver blade." For effect, he slid the scabbard down to show the smooth edge of the glinting metal.

"I've never seen anything like it," Jax murmured, fascinated by the object. "I didn't realize their horns could be used legally." She was alluding to the blissful magic unicorns embodied.

Antoine wagged a finger. "Once the horn is separated from the beast, the magic disappears. Believe me though, sometimes I wish this lulled me into an idyllic oblivion." He flipped the weapon skillfully in the air, catching it with one hand.

Jax pondered the dagger a moment longer, realizing there was something else battering away in the back of her mind. "Did you hear about the unfortunate accident one of Duke Mensina's messenger boys encountered?" The news her grandfather shared that first day flooded her mind. She remembered how the accident upset the crotchety old man, surprising her at the time. Where was this compassion with his own granddaughter? "I believe it was the young man who delivered your invitation to the feast. He was returning home from Beautraud."

Antoine's eyes darkened with sadness. "No, I hadn't heard. That's terrible. What a way to go, to be run through by such a beautiful creature."

Jax parted her lips to agree, but a menacing realization made her words catch in her throat. She hadn't mentioned that a unicorn impaled the young boy, or even that he'd been killed. A wave of terror surged through her veins, but she forced herself to meet the knight's somber expression. Fearing words would betray her, she nodded, hoping Antoine would assume her sudden change in demeanor was due to her sorrow for the deceased lad. A young man whose death had been overlooked, presumably dying from a wild animal attack. Her mind now raced as the pieces began to fall into place. The page boy, unbeknownst to everyone, was the first victim of the Feast of Champions. The murder weapon that ended his life was mere inches away from her clenched hands, being fondled by what could only be a sadistic madman. Instead of fearing for her life, all she could think about was why. Why was the boy killed? How did his murder connect to those of Chalfant and the young woman?

Steeling herself for what was to come, Jax met Antoine's curious gaze, studying him carefully. And for the first time, she saw her answer, now realizing how foolish she'd been to be duped by the ultimate deception. She saw the truth in the man's eyes, not because she was good at reading people, but because of his very eyes. Their color. She'd always assumed they were a deep shade of amber, because that was the eye color noblemen of the realm always had. A bit on the dark side, yes, but amber all the same. Now, as she looked at him closely, she cursed her foolhardy assumption. The man staring back at her had brown eyes. Regular, common folk brown eyes. This man was not Sir Antoine of House Wincaester.

"This feast has been plagued with many unfortunate deaths," she finally spoke, sounding nonchalant. "I know my grandfather wanted to keep them under wraps for fear of tarnishing the festival's reputation, but a man died the very first night of the tournament. The night you revealed yourself as the Knight with No Face," Jax added pointedly, although she was careful not to layer too much malice in her tone. Her companion's face remained uncaringly neutral, so she continued. "A man traveling with the Savant delegation. I've heard rumors it was murder." She paused only a moment, finally seeing a twitch in the man's muddy eyes. "Of course, the Ducal Guard found a dagger and torn piece of clothing at the scene, belonging to, you'll never guess—" she lowered her voice to a dramatic whisper— "Lord Pettraud! That's why I've been having to cover for him, because my future consort, Lord Pettraud, has been imprisoned for the poor man's murder." Jax rose from her seat, too caught up in the grips of unraveling the mystery to consider the danger of confronting the knight alone. "I've been spending my time here trying to figure out who would frame Perry for such a heinous crime, and the answer has been right beside me all along." She turned on a heel, facing this Knight with No Face with a vengeance. "You couldn't kill Chalfant with your unicorn dagger because that would be too suspicious. Having been bested by Lord Pettraud in the jousting match, you had to do something to protect your title as the legendary Knight with No Face, and what could be better than framing your final rival as a stone-cold killer? My grandfather's invitation to stay at the palace was the perfect opportunity, where you could simply slip into Perry's room, take his dagger and tunic, and place them at the scene of the crime. It was only a matter of time before Lord Pettraud was apprehended and you were off the hook. But then you overheard the Savant bannermen talking about a wayward woman who'd been a companion to Chalfant. Fearing that she would somehow link you to Chalfant's murder, you sought a girl fitting her description and strangled her, and because she was a tourney wench, no one bothered enough to care. You had been so careful, your tracks so perfectly covered by the seeming randomness of the crimes. Your only mistake was dropping your Shadow Seal in Lord Pettraud's closet." Jax stared triumphantly down at the shocked man. "You are not Sir Antoine

Wincaester of Beautraud, but a member of the Shadow Brethren, and Chalfant knew it. That's why you killed him. Because he had to be silenced. And when you learned he may have had a lover, you had to get rid of her, too, in case she also knew you were impersonating the Knight with No Face." Jax stopped, her bravado failing as she watched the thug stand up, his face a contortion of pure rage and hatred. "But why did you kill the page boy?"

The man before her began clapping, a menacing smirk spreading across his lips. "But you're so smart, Duchess. Can't you figure it out?" He moved closer, his once kind eyes now revealing a deadly threat. "The page boy delivered the missive to the real Sir Antoine. It wasn't even until my men and I raided and killed Wincaester's delegation that we even knew about the Feast of Champions. Once I pulled the invitation off the man's cold, dead body, the idea formed. The Knight with No Face was going to be awarded a fortune for his performance in the tournament, and since no one knew who he really was, I could ride here on his prissy little horse and collect it for myself. Of course, to cover my tracks, I sent word that I would be retiring from the knights' tourney circuit, just so I wouldn't have to display my lack of physical prowess and blow the cover of my ingenious ruse. We found the boy a day later and dispatched of him, confident that no one would be the wiser, given my unique unicorn dagger." He twirled the gleaming pearl hilt in the air, the moonlight catching the exposed silver blade. "Once I learned Chalfant was here, I knew he had to go. He and I had a brief run in back when he did a knight's residency in Beautraud. He was the only one here who could contradict my claim to the Wincaester name. Sir Antoine had always been such a shut-in, no one from the neighboring duchies would know him from a hole in the wall. A brilliantly executed plan, if I do say so myself."

Jax folded her arms, growing nervous at the rustling bushes behind the imposter's towering frame. She prayed his associates were not somehow following them. "Except for the part where I uncovered what you've been doing." She forced herself to stall, in the hopes one of her aunts would notice she'd gone missing from the ball.

Shrugging, the deviant grinned. "I can easily rectify this new predicament. With the deaths of your beloved parents so fresh, you just couldn't take the pressures of life." He lunged forward and forcefully grabbed her arm, dragging his blade tauntingly along the skin of her wrist. "I'm sure no one will even think twice about you taking your own life."

Plunging through a nearby rosebush, Perry launched himself to tackle the imposter, but not before Jax raised her knee and swiftly kicked the rogue between the legs. Howling like a wounded puppy, the faux Sir Antoine Wincaester crumbled to the ground, only to be pinned by a shredded and bleeding Perry. Captain Solomon and his men appeared out of thin air, wrestling with the murderous criminal, while Jax's grandfather helped a breathless Perry to his feet.

Staring at her savior in astounded delight, she wasn't sure if she was happier that he'd come to her rescue or that he was finally free of his dungeon prison. "Oh, Perry!" She threw her arms around his neck, crushing her body into his.

Chapter Eleven

Captain Solomon commanded his men to bring the imposter to Captain Roche and round up his henchmen, still camped out on the fairgrounds. "Thank goodness we got here when we did." The Captain of the Ducal Guard looked ashamed he had left his Duchess to face the danger alone.

"Well, it seems like Jacqueline can handle herself just fine," Duke Mensina growled proudly, giving his granddaughter a reassuring squeeze on the shoulder.

"How did you know I was in trouble?" Jax asked eagerly, her eyes still on a wondrously freed Perry.

"I went to the ducal treasury, only to find your grandfather just as he was leaving for the ball," Captain Solomon explained. "He had wrapped up a meeting with Sir Wincaester. The Knight with No Face requested his prize money in full, as he did not plan to stay around until the end of the tournament."

"The whelp said he was anxious to return home, now that his retirement was official. Considering I'd already gotten what I wanted out of his appearance, I figured I could arrange to have the gold transferred now and thought nothing of it. One less thing for me to worry about, as he so eloquently argued." Duke Mensina snorted in disbelief, no doubt annoyed at himself for falling for the ruse. "He signed the proper paperwork and I approved the prize money to be delivered to his suite tomorrow morning."

"When I arrived at the treasury, I showed the Duke the Shadow Seal and told him that we believed someone was paying the guild to sabotage Perry," Captain Solomon stated, his cheeks coloring slightly.

"Yes, I am going to look past the fact that you thought I might be behind this," Duke Mensina said, looking into his granddaughter's guilty eyes, "because, considering my past plots with your father, you had every right as a Duchess to be suspicious of my intentions."

Jax was surprised by the genuine sincerity in the familial violet eyes staring down at her.

"Once Captain Solomon showed me the seal," her grandfather said, "I knew something was amiss. The handwriting on the treasury paperwork Sir Wincaester filled out was the same writing as 'LeDuke' etched on the back of the crest."

"We found Captain Roche, who informed us that LeDuke is the name of an infamous member of the Shadow Brethren, wanted for several murders across a handful of duchies. We immediately sent men to find the imposter, while Duke Mensina and I went to release Perry," her ducal guardsman explained, smiling at the bedraggled young lord.

Perry grinned sheepishly. "While I was locked up, I kept trying to think why Sir Wincaester bothered me so much. I mean, any man would have to be out of his mind not to try to flirt with you, Jax, but there was something else about him that rubbed me the wrong way. Then, this afternoon, it hit me. I remembered seeing his likeness posted on a notice board in a town we rode through on our way here.

The rogue was wanted for ransacking an estate or something along those lines. I was fooled by the pageantry of the Knight with No Face to think that they could be one in the same person, but in the depths of my mind, doubt festered."

"We were all fooled by him, myself the most." She looked grimly across the garden, her eyes lingering on the bench she'd been sharing with the criminal mere moments before. "I was so quick to be charmed by him, simply because of his title. You'd think I would have learned by now that you can't trust anyone in this position."

"I refuse to let you be that jaded, Jax. You can't simply stop trusting people. Not when there are so many around you who care for you deeply." Perry moved to her side, allowing her to take in the view of Captain Solomon and her grandfather, with her aunts, Uma, and Hendrie breathlessly arriving in the garden clearing, concern for her written all over their faces.

Taking Perry's hand, she allowed a tearful smile to shine in the moonlight.

✝

Teaming up, Captain Roche's men were able to round up LeDuke's henchmen with the help of the Saphire Ducal Guard. Seven other wanted men were dragged into the depths of the palace dungeons, LeDuke's screams of rage echoing through the halls. Duke Mensina sent word immediately to the Duke of Beautraud and to House Wincaester to let them know of the developments.

Jax's heart ached for the family, knowing they would soon learn their beloved Antoine had been killed by the monster LeDuke. She and her grandfather had already arranged for the Knight with No Face's tournament winnings to benefit the charities of which Sir Antoine was a patron. LeDuke had done his research thoroughly, for every word about the knight's philanthropic background was found to be true.

After the foul start to the Feast of Champions, the Duke of Mensina could not hide the nefarious goings-on from his people any longer. The next morning, he preached from the tourney arena the evils of the Shadow Brethren and how Mensina and Saphire would jointly lead a new initiative to eradicate the criminal guild across the Realm of Virtues. Jax stood beside him, her presence calm and reassuring, a contrast to her grandfather's fiery propaganda. Rumors ran wild that she singlehandedly thwarted the imposter, and the public's awe and respect of her doubled overnight.

With all that transpired, Jax was happiest to have Perry back, his handsome figure appearing seemingly out of nowhere the minute she needed an arm to grasp or a confident smile to reassure her nerves. She couldn't believe how good-natured he'd been about the whole ordeal, continually showering praise on her for her bravery.

"I'm glad to have you back," she said as she clasped his hand and held it to her cheek during a rare moment alone. "I thought I'd done something that cooled your affection toward me." She lowered her eyes nervously to the ground.

"Whatever do you mean?" Perry asked, astonished.

"It's just that you seemed angry with me or something. The first night we were here, right before the joust, your attitude was so cold." She shuddered at the memory. "Then you ignored me all through dinner, and that brute's flirting only made things worse." She heaved her shoulders, uncomfortable just thinking about it. "The next morning you hardly glanced at me, and then you were thrown in the dungeons before I could figure out why."

Perry gave her a bemused grin, the sunset caressing his dark, curly hair. "Is that why you wanted to clear my name? So you could interrogate me yourself?"

"No." Jax rolled her eyes in blatant exasperation.

Chuckling, Perry drew her in closely, his arms circling her

slender body. "Oh Jax, I forget how incredibly perceptive you are. No, I was not having second thoughts about us in the very least. I suppose I should have told you sooner, but this festival happens to mark a year since my mother passed away," he shared, his eyes going misty. "The palace staff had placed some fresh flowers in my room the day we arrived. They were begonias, my mother's favorite. It put me in a bit of a sad mood, seeing them there. At the joust, I got to thinking how much I wish she'd lived to see me make someone as special as you proud." Even now, his handsome face was marred with grief. "I was lost in my own sorrows, I guess. I'm sorry, I should have let you in."

She had no words for her darling knight. A simple kiss said it all.

Chapter Twelve

Over the remaining days of the festival, Duke Mensina nearly bent over backward to express his deepest regrets at being so hotheaded and blind to Perry's innocence. Of course, Perry knew he had the upper hand, but he was as chivalrous as ever, using the opportunity to help Jax and her grandfather mend their strained relationship. "Family is everything in this life, Jax," Perry told her. "Royal, noble, or common blood, it's a love that runs deep." Despite the thorns that littered their familial past, Jax knew Perry was right. For her to truly prosper, both personally and as Duchess, she needed her family's strength behind her.

The morning of the Saphire delegation's departure came at last, souvenirs of the final feast still lingering in Jax's veins. She perhaps drank a bit too much honeyed mead the previous evening, her head aching at the rap on her chamber door. Uma giggled as she entered, having no sympathy for Jax's moaning complaints. She set to work packing the Duchess's belongings, laying out a simple traveling gown for the carriage ride back to Saphire. "We'll be leaving without you, Your Grace," Uma teased, placing a damp, cool towel on the Duchess's forehead.

"Good. I need a few more days to recover." Jax buried her head in her feather pillow, sulking at the prospect of spending hours sitting on a bumpy, uncomfortable bench.

With reluctance, she allowed her lady's maid to help her dress, and she soon was on her way to the palace entrance, a slew of palace staff in tow with her luggage.

"Let's not wait until the next imposter comes along to get together," Amia said with a chuckle, hugging Jax tightly. Each of her remaining aunts then took their turn to say goodbye.

"Yes, I hope there will be another occasion for us to celebrate. A wedding, perhaps?" Annette's eyebrows wiggled suggestively, her gaze dashing back and forth between Perry and Jax.

Laughing, Jax gathered Annette in a warm hug. "Whatever the occasion, you are always welcome in Saphire." She turned to Duke Mensina, giving him a kiss on the cheek. "That goes for you as well, Grand-Père." No trace of disdain lingered; her pet name for him was now spoken with genuine affection. He, in turn, hugged her close.

"Don't go getting into too much trouble now, Jacqueline," he playfully grumbled, yet a glimmer of concern sparkled in his eyes.

Jax gazed sheepishly at her beloved companions. Uma, Captain Solomon, and Perry each suppressed a snort of laughter. "No promises, Grand-Père. One never knows when trouble might pop up."

~BONUS CONTENT~

This edition features the Realm of Virtues story, **A Present Predicament***. This tale provides readers with an enchanting glimpse into the first Yuletide shared by Duchess Jacqueline and Lord Pettraud following the events of* **A Feast Most Foul.** *As the holiday season unfolds, they navigate a series of unexpected challenges and delightful surprises, shedding light on their burgeoning relationship and revealing the warmth and complexities of their bond.*

A Present Predicament

~A Realm of Virtues Story~

Sarah E. Burr

Chapter One

"Excuse me, Miss Uma? Might I have a word?"

Lord Percival Pettraud had clearly startled the young woman, for she leaped back from the pile of dresses she'd been sorting, her hand flying to her chest.

"Virtues, my lord, you gave me quite a fright."

Perry's cheeks warmed as he waited for the petite lady's maid to compose herself. "Apologies. I should have knocked."

"Before entering the private chambers of the Duchess of Saphire? Yes, that would probably be wise in the future." Uma Dorrow gave him a polite curtsy, although a smirk twisted on her lips.

Perry ran a hand through his thick, dark curls. "I'm still learning the ropes, I'm afraid. As the lowly seventh son of a Duke, royal etiquette wasn't seen as a priority for me."

Uma turned back to her work, sifting through the elaborate gowns lying across one of the plush sofas. "I don't think it's *royal* etiquette to knock on a lady's bedchamber before entering, my lord."

Perry's jaw went slack. Was meek, mild-mannered Uma actually *teasing* him? In the eight or so months he had been living at the Saphirian palace, she had always acted like a timid shadow. Where was this spritely spirit coming from?

Uma must have read his thoughts, for her cheeks colored, and she began to sputter. "It-it is my turn to beg forgiveness, Lord Pettraud. The Duchess asked me to help her sample some cordials for the grand Yuletide gala. The gingerbread malt seems to have made me quite bold."

Perry laughed, waving her apology aside. "Then I must be sure to seek it out. I'll need plenty of courage of my own to survive the night."

Uma tilted her head, clearly intrigued by his comment.

Perry continued for her benefit, "High Courtier Jaquobie has repeatedly informed me of the importance of the evening." He shuddered at his memory of the most recent encounter. "It seems all eyes will be on me to see if I am suitable to be the Duchess of Saphire's...companion." Perry almost choked on the last word. Not that he was disgusted by it, but because he was still in a blissful state of disbelief that Jacqueline Arienta Xavier, the intelligent and engaging Duchess of Saphire, would one day become his wife...that is if he didn't embarrass himself in front of the Saphirian high lords and ladies.

Uma cleared her throat. "Were you looking for the Duchess, Lord Pettraud?"

Perry realized he was likely keeping the young woman from her duties with his rambling. "No, I was looking for you." He looked around the beautifully decorated sitting area. "I was wondering if you might help me with a little mission."

"Mission, my lord?" Uma's nose wrinkled, and she nervously tucked a strand of loose, mousey brunette hair back behind her ear.

"Oh, nothing dangerous. I'm simply inquiring what Duchess Jacqueline might like for a Yuletide gift. I'd like to give her something special, something that she can use." Perry's gaze dropped to the polished stone floor. He felt devious for asking, as he'd already arranged for a present. He was merely there to ensure the gift remained a surprise. No doubt, Uma would inform her Duchess that Perry had stopped by inquiring about ideas, thus putting Jax off the trail. At least, he hoped so. Jax did have an uncanny knack for solving the trickiest of puzzles.

At his question, Uma chuckled. "A challenge, for sure, my lord. What do you get a woman who has everything?"

"Ah, so you can see what I'm up against?" Perry grinned. With her guard down, Uma was a delightful young woman. He could see why his longtime valet and friend, Hendrie, had taken a liking to her.

Uma tapped her chin in thought. "Indeed. Although, I'm not sure I'll be able to help you, Lord Pettraud. I think…" she paused, looking back over her shoulder at the closed doors to Jax's bedroom. "I think as long as you don't give her some old tome reeking of leather, you'll be fine. High Courtier Jaquobie and her council of advisors presented the Duchess with several history books as a Yuletide offering only just this morning. As if she'd want to do *more* reading outside of her work." Uma chuckled. "The Duchess really put her acting skills to the test. I almost believed she was an ardent book lover."

Perry did his best to join in Uma's laughter, but inside, his heart sank. A leather tome? It was just his luck. The one thing Jax wouldn't want was the one thing he'd gotten her.

Chapter Two

Bidding Uma a hurried goodbye, Perry dashed out into the hallway of the residential wing of the Saphirian palace.

"Virtues," he mumbled to himself as he began to stalk back to his private apartment, "Yuletide is only a day away. How am I supposed to come up with another present before tomorrow's gala?" He ran a hand through his hair in frustration. He had thought he'd come up with the perfect gift, something not only meant for enjoyment but meaningful to them both.

Perry had spent the last few months secretly compiling different accounts from Jax's companions regarding their thrilling summer visit to the Duchy of Mensina earlier that year. At the Feast of Champions, a knight had been found dead in his tent, and Perry was accused of his murder. Jax had thrown herself into the investigation to clear Perry's name and see justice done, even going so far as to confront the killer herself. For a Yuletide gift, Perry had written a detailed account of the adventure, interviewing Hendrie, Uma, and the Ducal Guard to describe the events that had taken place while he'd been imprisoned in the Mensina dungeons. In order to keep the book a complete surprise, Perry's informants all believed he was writing a report to send home to his father, the Duke of Pettraud. Once he had written and illustrated the harrowing tale, painting Jax as the fierce and brilliant heroine that she was, Perry had enlisted the services of a Saphirian master crafter to bind the book for him in ornamented leather.

Uma's glib words battered around his mind. It wasn't that he was giving Jax a dusty *old* tome. But it was still a book…one newly made and sure to smell of the violet-dyed leather he'd selected while visiting the crafter's shop.

Perry sighed. Maybe he could find Jax something else in the Saphirian marketplace after he picked up the book from the crafter's that afternoon. But what to get the woman who had everything?

Lost in his troubled thoughts, Perry ambled back to his suite.

"Now, where is your Yuletide spirit?"

A musical voice dissolved his gloomy mood, and a grin twisted onto Perry's lips as he turned toward the welcome sound.

"Much better." Jax laughed as she glided toward him.

She looked lovely in a dark gray riding habit, her long, caramel waves plaited and pinned up under a smart, stylish hat.

"Back from a ride?" Perry wished she had invited him along. Exploring the palace grounds with her was one of his favorite pastimes.

Jax sighed. "Heading out, I'm afraid." She pulled a black glove off one of her elegant hands before taking hold of his. "I'm off to catch the Yuletide bounty."

Perry nodded. Jax had explained the lovely holiday tradition to him earlier in the week. Every Yuletide, Jax's father, the late Duke Richard Xavier, had embarked on a grand fishing expedition, donating his entire bounty to a Saphirian village's Yuletide feast. As Saphire's Duchess, Jax had taken up the mantle herself and would be spending the day fishing on Lake Saltrine.

"Is everything all right?" Perry examined Jax's refined features. She seemed uneasy; her beautiful amethyst eyes were tight with worry.

She sighed, the corner of her lip curling in a sheepish smile. "I'm usually not so transparent."

"You don't have to wear your regal mask around me, Jax." Perry placed a gentle palm on her forearm. "Is there anything I can do to help?"

Her gaze dropped to his hand for a moment. "Just your being here is enough." Her expression glowed with gratitude.

Underneath his tunic collar, Perry's neck warmed. She really was the most dazzling creature he had ever laid eyes upon. Jax often left him in a euphoric daze with her wit, charm, and intelligence.

When Perry had first been informed that Duke Richard and Duke Cornelius Pettraud had arranged Perry and Jax's marriage, he'd been suspiciously hesitant and downright appalled. He and Jax had both been ambushed with the news over a state dinner shortly after Jax's coronation. It hadn't surprised Perry to learn about the life-altering arrangement through a junior Pettraudian courtier. His father couldn't even have been bothered to inform Perry himself ahead of his visit to Saphire. But Perry had been taken aback that he'd been the Pettraud son selected for this arrangement. Growing up, as the youngest of seven sons, Duke Pettraud had rarely shown Perry any kindness, so why start now? At the time, Perry had assumed his father was using him as a simple bargaining chip, sending him off to marry some cold, uncaring woman for Pettraud's own political gain. Perry had heard stories about Jacqueline's beauty but not much about the strength of her character. Yet, after being in her company for only a short while, his entire outlook regarding his father's decision had changed. With her, Perry could see a bright, happy future. A future he dared hope to dream about.

Of course, that future currently remained undecided. Since Jax had not been aware of the arrangement made by her father and Duke Pettraud, she had been quite stunned to learn about it from one of Duke Pettraud's junior courtiers. Perry would have even gone so far as to say she was disappointed, heartbroken that her father had done this without her consent. Yet, Jax put on a brave face and welcomed Perry into her home under the condition that they would spend an extended period getting to know each other before an engagement was announced. At the time, Perry couldn't help but wonder if Jax had been simply delaying things until she could find a way *out* of the marriage agreement. In her, Perry saw a kindred spirit. She wanted to marry for love, just like he did. Although, their situation suited Perry just fine. He was certain he had fallen in love with her the moment she called him "Perry" for the first time.

He gazed at her now, desperate to make her feel better. "Are you worried the fish will prove too elusive for your nets?" Since the spoils of the Yuletide bounty went to a village in need, he imagined Jax was feeling the pressure to perform well.

At his concern, Jax snorted. "I am a very skilled fisherman, thank you very much. I've participated in the expedition for many years now." Her teasing words softened. "It's just…this will be the first time in a long, long while that Papa hasn't been at my side."

Perry's heart tightened at the sadness pooling in her eyes. This would be the first Yuletide without her beloved parents. "Your father will always be at your side, Jax." Perry lifted a hand to his heart. "In here."

A lone tear fell onto her cheek. "My heart feels quite empty at the moment."

Her admission touched him. Jax was usually so closed off regarding her feelings. Without thinking, he gathered her into his arms, wordlessly offering her comfort and understanding.

She tensed at his affectionate touch but soon pressed her cheek against his chest. They stood there for a time without speaking.

A throat cleared at the end of the corridor. "Ahem, Duchess? Sorry to bother you. The envoy to the lake is ready."

Perry and Jax parted, their attention turning in unison to the armored figure at the end of the hall. Captain George Solomon of the Ducal Guard stood, a sheepish expression on his face.

"Nonsense, George. I'm sorry to have kept everyone waiting." Jax's features smoothed into her regal mask, a façade Perry had become quite familiar with by now. He could practically see her barricading her emotions and weaknesses away from the world.

George dipped his head in response, clearly embarrassed to have interrupted a private moment between the two of them.

He does it often enough, you'd think he'd be used to it, Perry grumbled to himself.

Jax turned to Perry, a bright, endearing smile settling onto her lips once more. "I shall see you when I return victorious, Lord Pettraud."

Perry laughed at the theatrical bravado she displayed. "I'm sure you will capture every fish in the lake, Duchess."

As she hurried toward George, Perry gazed after her longingly. *Just as you have captured my heart, Jax.*

Chapter Three

"Are you sure, Perry?" Hendrie scratched at his straw-colored hair. "I don't mind riding down to the city square myself."

Perry batted the comment away. "Please, I need a distraction."

A knock sounded from the entrance to Perry's apartment.

Perry shot a questioning glance at Hendrie. With Jax gone for the day, who could be on the other side?

Hendrie moved quickly to the door and opened it.

High Courtier Jaquobie stood in the doorway, his hands clenched in front of him in a pensive manner.

"High Courtier." Perry struggled to sound friendly. The thin, spindly man unnerved him a great deal. "What brings you by?"

"I hope I am not interrupting." Jaquobie strode into the sitting area of Perry's suite, eyeing the saddlebags seated on one of the sofas. "Planning a trip, Lord Pettraud?"

Perry shook his head. "Hendrie and I were just getting ready to ride into Sephretta. Duchess Jacqueline has told me the marketplace is a holiday marvel this time of year."

Jaquobie stroked his long, pointy black beard. "Lovely." His nasal tone did not sound lovely at all.

"May I help you with something, High Courtier?" Perry wrung his hands. Usually, Jax was around to deflect the shrewd man's attention.

"I wanted to speak to you about the importance of the Yuletide gala."

Perry swallowed. "Again?" Did Jaquobie think him some unruly child? He was twenty-eight years old, for Virtues' sake.

"The High Lords of Saphire have Duchess Jacqueline's ear. If any of them feel that you are not up to the task of Prince Consort, well…" Jaquobie motioned a flippant hand toward the door.

Perry folded his arms. "High Courtier, I find it hard to believe you would allow Saphire to break an agreement made with the Duchy of Pettraud." He hated that his relationship with Jax boiled down to an "agreement" in so many people's eyes, but he spoke in terms a man like Jaquobie would understand.

Jaquobie scoffed at his bold statement. "As crude as this may sound, the agreement made by your father was made with a dead man. Duchess Jacqueline is the sovereign of Saphire now. The only reason she is upholding her late father's arrangement is out of respect. To both Duke Richard *and* Duke Pettraud."

Perry stilled, barely believing Jaquobie spoke so frankly with him.

"Which is why Duchess Jacqueline would have no objection from me, should she choose to dissolve the agreement *if* she deemed it in Saphire's best interests." Jaquobie's dark amber eyes narrowed pointedly before the man sighed. "If you want this marriage to come to fruition, I cannot stress enough the importance of impressing the high lords and ladies of Saphire. Jacqueline is very fond of you, Lord Pettraud, but if you are not strong enough to stand by her side, she will put duty before her own heart. She's done it before."

Perry took several steeling breaths, processing Jaquobie's curious words. While they had been harsh, the High Courtier had spoken plainly about what needed to be done to win Jax's hand in marriage. "I appreciate your candor, High Courtier. Please know your words of wisdom will not be dismissed."

A mischievous twinkle flashed in Jaquobie's cunning gaze. "I'll leave you to enjoy your day, Lord Pettraud. Although, I might suggest you stop by the library while visiting the capital. It houses an extensive collection on the Saphirian noble families who will be attending the gala. It might prove useful." With a dip of his chin, Jaquobie departed the chamber.

Hendrie locked the door behind the man and leaned against it with a sigh. "Would Duchess Xavier do that? Would she really break the pact made by her father?"

Perry forced a confident smile. "Not without good reason. And believe me, I have no plans to give her one."

Putting Jaquobie's chilly encounter behind them, Hendrie helped Perry into his riding clothes, and by late morning, the two were on their way to the stables.

"Virtues, Hendrie, even the snow is brighter in Saphire, isn't it?" Perry stared in awe at the sprawling grounds that lay between them and the palace stables. Having grown up in the dreary confines of his family's formidable, gloomy castle, Perry was continually enchanted by the ethereal beauty he had encountered in Saphire.

"Greetings, Lord Pettraud."

Perry had been so engrossed by the snow-covered landscape, he had failed to see a senior member of the Ducal Guard approach until now.

"Corporal Highriver." The broad-shouldered man supplied his name when Perry didn't immediately respond.

"How is the season treating you, Corporal?" Perry asked, ashamed he hadn't remembered the warrior's name, despite having been introduced to him before. The Corporal had served the Ducal Guard since Jax was a young girl, and she was quite fond of the gruff soldier. Perry could almost feel the phantom drip of Jaquobie's disapproval down his spine. If he was to be the Prince Consort Jax deserved, he should start by taking a more active interest in those around her.

"Very well, thank you." Highriver nodded a greeting to Hendrie. "You look like you're about to set off for a ride. Do you require an escort, my lord?"

Perry shook his head. "Oh, no. I'm just off to the Sephretta marketplace for a bit of holiday cheer."

Highriver frowned. "I must insist you take an escort, my lord. It's not safe for you to travel alone."

"I won't be alone." Perry patted Hendrie on the shoulder. "We've made the trek before, Corporal. No need to bother any of the Ducal Guard."

Highriver shifted his weight to his back foot, revealing more clearly the empty sleeve hanging lifelessly from his side. Perry didn't know the story behind the injury that had cost the man his arm and respectfully avoided his gaze.

"Ah, but the fresh snowfall has a way of toying with one's mind, my lord."

"As a Knight of Pettraud, I am *aware*." Perry immediately regretted his sharp, clipped tone, but after the tongue lashing he had received from Jaquobie, he'd grown quite tired of everyone in Saphire assuming him incompetent.

Highriver bowed his head, chastened. "Forgive me, my lord. I meant no offense." He gave them both a curt smile. "Enjoy your ride."

Perry debated calling the man back over and apologizing, but before he could make up his mind, Highriver disappeared into the ducal gardens.

"That could have gone better, mate," Hendrie whispered, his brown gaze trailing after the distinguished soldier.

Perry tugged his cloak a bit tighter. "I know, I know." His mood darkened. Between Jax's gift, Jaquobie's visit, and his encounter with Highriver, the day was not going in his favor.

As if sensing his sour spirits, Hendrie puffed out his chest as they resumed walking toward the stables. "I think I shall ask the Duchess's lady's maid to the Yuletide gala."

Perry cocked an eyebrow. "Really? Do you think you'll be able to get a word out? You always get quite tongue-tied around her." He ribbed his valet with an elbow.

Hendrie turned the color of a holly berry. "I-I do not."

"Well, mate, you better get a move on. The ball *is* tomorrow." Perry patted Hendrie's shoulder. "Who's to say she doesn't already have some fine suitor escorting her?"

Hendrie paled. "You think? She didn't mention she was going with anyone when we spoke at dinner last night."

Perry shrugged, enjoying his role of antagonist. So often, Hendrie was the one teasing him about his shortcomings.

Hendrie gnawed nervously on his lip as he looked back over his shoulder toward the castle.

"Why don't you go ask her now?" Perry suggested, a sneaky idea brewing in his mind.

"Now?" Hendrie stopped in his tracks. "What about going into Sephretta? If we don't leave now, we might not make it back before nightfall."

Perry waved a hand. "No worries, Hendrie. I can ride into town myself and collect Jax's gift."

Hendrie glared at his charge. "You heard what Corporal Highriver said. The trails can get confusing in the snow."

"And you heard what *I* said," Perry countered. "I know a thing or two about riding through the winter woods. And what's more," he said, motioning to the vast landscape, "all I'll be doing is following the road. It couldn't be any easier."

Hendrie's gaze was filled with doubt.

Perry sighed. "Would it make you rest easier if I asked Corporal Highriver to find me an escort?"

"It would."

"Fine." Perry hiked his saddlebag up further on his shoulder. "I'll go track him down. Now, *you* go find your lady love and woo her into attending the gala with you."

Hendrie grinned. "Thanks, Perry." With a chipper salute, Hendrie took off toward the castle, a bounce in his step.

Perry waited for Hendrie to disappear behind the snow-dusted hedges lining the inner courtyard before turning around and resuming his journey toward the stables.

While he didn't enjoy lying to Hendrie, Perry didn't need some member of the Ducal Guard traipsing after him. The time alone would serve him well to mentally prepare for the Yuletide trials ahead. As a very capable rider, he could follow the road into the capital without issue. He *was* a Knight of Pettraud, after all.

Chapter Four

As the capital city of Sephretta came into view, Perry marveled at the picturesque, wintry scene. The tiled rooftops were covered in freshly fallen snow, soft flurries still dancing through the air all around. Massive wreaths adorned the gates to the city, welcoming the approach of Yuletide. As Perry neared, he slowed his mount, taking in the sight. Unlike his homeland of Pettraud, known for its impenetrable fog, Sephretta was bathed in bright light, even amidst the snow flurries.

At the gates of the city, he dismounted from his horse, maneuvering amongst the crowd milling about. It had been ages since he had wandered in anonymity. Even as the lowly seventh son of House Pettraud, Perry had still been confined to a castle growing up, surrounded by guards and servants. Rarely did he ever get to venture out on his own, and freedom had become even more elusive since arriving in Saphire. Jax took his security very seriously, and he rarely could go anywhere without some kind of escort. To have been able to shake Hendrie today…well, it had been a stroke of devious luck.

After securing his horse at the entrance stables, Perry tossed his saddlebag over his shoulder and began to wander into the heart of the city. Garlands and pine wreaths peppered doors and windows, crimson candles shining their light brightly in Yuletide wonder. Against the canvas of falling snow, it was a beautiful, charming sight. Perfect for one of his paintings. Perhaps while he was in town, he would stock up on some new colors to capture the scene.

Recalling his last visit here to meet with the master craftsman, Perry navigated the busy streets, doing his best to remain invisible. He kept the hood of his cloak low, partially obscuring his lavender-colored eyes from the crowd. His eyes declared his royal heritage, and he had no desire to have the public fawning over him. Word had begun to spread that a Prince of Pettraud had come to court Duchess Jacqueline, and any passersby would likely be able to put two and two together if they saw him strolling around the Saphirian capital. Given that he was on his own, he knew it would be tempting the Virtues to flaunt his presence in the city square.

Delicious smells of sugar and cinnamon caught his attention, his stomach rumbling. The ride into town had taken little over an hour, as Perry had enjoyed a leisurely trot, admiring the forest lining the well-worn road. If he had enough time after meeting with the crafter, perhaps he'd stop by a tearoom or bakery for an afternoon snack.

‡

"Ah, Lord Pettraud. Good to see you, sir."

Perry closed the door behind him, letting the warm, earthy air of the master crafter's shop wash over him. He smiled at Edgard Gurns, the owner and proprietor, as he lowered his hood. "Am I that obvious?" Inwardly, he cringed. He thought he had worn a subtle disguise.

Gurns chuckled and pointed to the saddlebag slung over Perry's shoulder. "You purchased that the last time you were here. I never forget one of my wares."

At that, Perry's shoulders loosened in relief. "It's a fine piece of equipment. Likely to outlast everything else I own."

Gurns patted the stained apron covering his portly middle. "I couldn't call myself a master crafter if it didn't."

Perry surveyed the empty shop. "How's business?"

"I can't complain, although the weather today has driven customers home early, it seems. With the snow we've had of late, folks are needing their leather shoes repaired and the like."

"Good, steady work," Perry commented, unable to imagine what it might be like to spend one's days fixing shoes.

Gurns rubbed his hands together. "Boring work more like it. Unlike our little project. Would you like to see it, my lord?"

Perry's stomach flipped. He had been so excited to see how the book turned out when he awoke this morning. Now, he prayed he could summon the skill to force enthusiasm. "By all means."

Gurns leaned down behind his workbench and returned with a large, burlap wrapping. Placing it on the table, he slowly lifted the cloth back to reveal what lay bundled inside.

"Virtues." Perry's eyes grew wide at the violet cover, the title he'd selected etched in shining, shimmering gold. Gurns had stitched gold and silver thread along the edges of the binding, pairing together the regal colors of Saphire and Pettraud in a beautiful yet simple way. Under the title, the master crafter had embedded a small amethyst gemstone and an emerald Perry had procured, another symbol of Jax's and Perry's duchies. The jewels were framed in gold plating, capturing every ounce of light the shop offered. Perry didn't have to fake his amazement at the fine craftsmanship. "Gurns, old boy, this is a masterpiece."

The man beamed at Perry, his cheeks reddening with pride. "Aye, Lord Pettraud, you're pulling my leg."

Perry shook his head. "Believe me, I have seen many treasures in my day, but nothing so magnificent as this." His heart lurched into his throat as he took in the novel he'd written and illustrated. What would Jax think of it? Would she see the time and love that had gone into its creation, or would she see it as just another book to add to her growing pile?

Chapter Five

The smell of parchment overwhelmed his senses as Perry stepped into the foyer of the grand library. Situated in the heart of the capital, the Library of Saphire was one of the oldest archives in the realm. Jax had taken him here once, but only in passing. Today would be the first time Perry made use of the library's extensive resources.

As he stood admiring the tall and seemingly endless rows of overflowing bookshelves, a robed scholar shuffled over to greet him. In no time at all, Perry was situated at a polished wooden table laden with research material.

"Excuse me, sir?" a raspy voice interrupted his reading a time later. "I'm afraid the library will be closing soon."

"Already?" Perry glanced up from his stack of books and scrolls, searching for a clock. Virtues, he'd been here for over three hours! He felt like he'd barely scratched the surface of his research.

The scholar nodded. "Normally, we remain open until well into the evening, but the snow is falling much more heavily now, and many of our scholars live outside the city walls."

"Of course, of course." Perry rose and began gathering all the books and documents he'd been reviewing. "I wouldn't want them to be snowed in on my account."

"Please, sir, you can leave your books here," the elder man shooed Perry away in typical scholarly fashion. "We'll take care of them in the morning."

Perry thanked the man for his assistance and grabbed his saddlebag. If the library was shutting down due to inclement weather, he'd better begin to make his way back to the palace and soon.

"I hope Jax's fishing expedition hasn't been hindered by the snow," Perry murmured to himself as he stepped outside once more into the cold air blanketing the marketplace.

Despite the handcrafted book nestled safely in his pack, Perry strolled through the marketplace with a watchful eye, examining the various wares being peddled. While part of him hoped Jax would appreciate the novel he'd written, Perry couldn't risk disappointing her.

It didn't help that Jaquobie's words still haunted his thoughts. Up until this morning, Perry had never seriously considered that Jax might break off the agreement made by their fathers. They cared for each other; of that he was certain. But Jax had been trained to put duty above her own desires. If he proved not worthy of the title Prince Consort, would she really send him home, regardless of her feelings?

As he made his way toward the stables to collect his horse, a glassmaker's stall caught his eye. The prismatic light sparkled like a beacon in the increasingly heavy snowfall. Perhaps he could find a trinket for Jax here and then give her the book at some later time.

"Looking for anything in particular, good sir?" the merchant purred, her accent Savantian.

"Something for a lady," Perry answered gruffly, making sure to keep his lavender gaze down whilst in public.

The merchant twirled a strand of long, dark hair. "A *special* lady?"

Perry nodded as he surveyed her wares. Decorative glass balls were hardly a suitable gift for a Duchess.

"Might I suggest this?" The merchant pulled forth a handheld mirror, framed in ornately molded glass. "The glass comes from Kwatalarian sand, the very last shipment to leave its borders before Duchess Amyra's embargo. Very rare. Very beautiful. Perfect for capturing the light to illuminate a lady's fine features."

Perry ran a finger along the long handle. The glass had been designed in the shape of a vine, ending with a blooming rose. He liked the idea of giving Jax's something unique, something no one else could give her. "I'll take it." He reached into his saddlebag bag and pulled out his coin purse. He would have just enough gold left after this to pay the stable hand for taking care of his horse.

His purchases tucked away in his saddlebag, Perry felt a glowing sense of accomplishment as he escorted his mare away from the city gates. The book had turned out better than he could ever have imagined. Perhaps he'd keep it for himself, as a souvenir of his time with Jax. The tome deserved to be appreciated. After his conversation with Uma, he feared if he gave it to Jax, it would just be hidden away in her library, never to be touched. The mirror would be a special enough gift. Who'd ever heard of glass made from Kwatalarian sand? Surely, Jax would be impressed.

During his time in the library, he'd also discovered a wealth of information about the Saphirian noble families and the duchy's traditions, although he knew there was still much to learn. Perry hoped the archives up at the palace might aid him further in his quest to learn more about his new home.

A gust of wind pelted wet snow onto his exposed skin. Pulling his hood tightly around his face, Perry shivered. Not only had the snow picked up, but the temperature had fallen quite drastically, as well. He opted to keep his saddlebag strapped to his back, the leather pressed against him keeping him warm. He climbed atop his horse and set out toward the palace, keeping to the main road. The snow had accumulated several inches, but he could make out a set of carriage tracks and used them as a guide.

He'd been on the road for nearly forty minutes when he heard voices up ahead of him. Through the thick, falling snow, an opulent carriage came into view, traveling in the same direction as he. Perry slowed his mount as he neared, wondering who could be traveling along the palace road in such refined luxury this time of day.

"I wish we had brought another footman along. Who will ride ahead and announce our arrival?" a high-pitched, whiny female voice rattled from inside the carriage.

Surprised he could hear the voices clearly, Perry spied smoke coming from the other side of the coach. Someone inside must be smoking a pipe with the window open.

"The Duchess's courtiers will announce us, my pigeon. Please, will you let me enjoy my leaf in peace?" A gravelly male voice floated through the air.

"We should have brought another footman, especially where we are staying at the palace overnight. What will the other nobles think?" the woman complained. "Rumor has it that this will be the most opulent gala in decades."

The man scoffed. "The Duchess is probably hoping all the glamor will distract the High Lords from the disastrous suitor at her side."

A chill ran down Perry's spine, and not from the cold.

"Ha!" the woman shrieked. "To think, the mighty Duchess of Saphire chained to a son of Pettraud."

"A *seventh* son, no less. He doesn't even have a title."

"What is she thinking?" the woman clucked. "I would have

broken the engagement the day it was revealed."

"Mind you, pigeon, she hasn't officially declared the two of them engaged. A wise move on her part. If I know Duchess Saphire, and I *do*, she's likely waiting for the poor sod to make a fool of himself so she can back out gracefully."

The woman giggled. "Well, this gala certainly just got more interesting, my pumpkin."

Perry yanked the reins of his horse, falling farther behind the carriage until he was out of earshot. He'd heard enough.

Snow peppered his face, mixing with the tears spilling from his eyes. The cruel words he'd just overheard spun viciously in his head. Disastrous suitor? Poor sod? These people didn't even know him, and they'd already declared him a failure, simply because he'd been born seventh in his family line.

He couldn't bear the sight of the carriage any longer, nor did he wish to ride by. Knowing these pompous fools, they'd think him rude for not stopping and introducing himself, and he didn't wish to give them any further fuel to use against him. With a hard tug of the reins, Perry urged his mount off the road. He was close enough to the castle grounds; he could travel the rest of the way through the forest.

Chapter Six

"A *seventh* son, no less."

Perry mimicked the high lord in an unflattering manner, picturing the speaker as a grotesque toad of a man. As he rode through the tranquil forest, Perry tried to push the unpleasant near encounter out of his mind, but out here all alone, he continued to stew over the harsh words. Did all the high lords and ladies of Saphire think him a hopeless case? That soon, he would be sent packing back to Pettraud, drenched in shame?

One thought clamored through the din raging inside his head. Had Jax been merely humoring him all these months, stringing him along until she could cut him loose?

"No," Perry snapped out loud, his voice echoing throughout the snowy woods. What he and Jax had was real...right?

Perry's horse snorted in retort, tossing her mane as she stumbled through a growing snowdrift. It was only then that Perry realized several more inches had accumulated. The snow fell steadily through the tree canopy, obscuring the sky above.

Perry slowed his mare, surveying the silent forest around him. The trees stretched on for miles in every direction. Without the sun guiding his path, he felt rather lost.

He gritted his teeth as he looked every which way, trying to regain his bearings. The snow had already made quick work of covering the horse's hoofprints, so he wasn't even sure which way he had ridden from.

"Virtues," he seethed. "I never should have left the road." He should have faced those pompous clowns head-on. Instead, he had retreated like a coward and gotten himself lost in unfamiliar territory. A Prince Consort worthy of Jax's heart would never have backed down from a challenge. Maybe those nobles in the carriage were right. Maybe he was hopeless.

A low growl shattered the serene peace of the forest. The hairs on the back of Perry's neck went rigid as his lavender gaze darted between the trees.

Another snarl echoed. Perry's mount danced nervously, the snow muffling her hooves.

Perry reached to stroke the horse's neck, whispering calm words of reassurance. His eyes never stopped tracking the shifting shadows within the forest. What creature had made such a beastly sound?

The growling continued, the vicious noises layering on top of one another. Whatever hunted him was not hunting alone.

Perry reached for his waist, where a sheathed sword normally would have hung…but not today. No, he had left his weapons at the palace, not expecting them to be needed for a simple ride into Sephretta. Virtues, what a Knight of Pettraud he was turning out to be.

He pushed his self-loathing subconscious into oblivion and focused on the situation at hand. Perry scanned the forest floor around them, searching for a large branch sticking out of the snow or anything that could be used as a weapon. He found nothing.

The growls were now accompanied by snapping jaws, the terrifying sounds growing closer by the moment. Desperate to protect himself and his mount, Perry yanked his saddlebag off his shoulder and rummaged around inside. His fingers brushed over the wrapped book before finding the cold, hard handle of the glass mirror. He seized onto it and pulled it from his satchel. With its clublike design, the mirror was better than nothing.

Securing his bag on his shoulder, Perry held the mirror out with his right arm, like a knight prepared to duel. The prismatic mirror captured the natural light illuminating the forest and sent beams of pretty colors across the snow.

The light reflected off the cool stare leering at him from the underbrush. A white wolf, its fur almost blending in perfectly with the snow, bared its fangs as it prowled forward.

Perry sized up the animal with a practiced eye. This beast was larger than any he had ever seen before in the wilds of Pettraud. And it was not alone. Two more wolves flanked either side, their colors a tawny brown. Despite being smaller than their leader, they were no less threatening.

Before Perry could properly react, his horse caught the scent of the predators and squealed in panic. The noise propelled the wolves forward, their jaws snapping as they pounced.

Perry urged the horse forward, the mare darting away just in nick of time. The white wolf's jaw only snagged the frosty air.

Perry's good fortune ended there. The tawny wolves rounded on the horse's front, sending the mare rearing. With only one hand holding the reins, Perry lost his grip and tumbled to the ground. He landed hard on the snow, a jolt shooting up his spine. Dazed, he shook his head and his focus cleared just as his horse took off into the depths of the woods, the tawny wolves giving chase.

The white wolf crouched a mere six feet in front of him, ready to pounce.

Perry scrambled to his feet, grappling for the mirror to defend himself. Dismay flooded through him as he snatched the trinket up from the ground. It had landed on a rock jutting out of the snow and snapped in two. He grabbed the handle, the broken glass where it had once held the head of the mirror now a sharp spike. With it, he just might stand a chance of wounding the creature.

Perry held the broken mirror handle in front of him like a dagger, doing his best to keep calm and focused. The wolf paced back and forth with its tongue lolled to one side of its mouth, seeming to relish Perry's fear.

Then, without warning, the wolf lunged for Perry's cloaked arm. Instinctively, Perry yanked his arm backward, causing his saddlebag to slip down his shoulder. The wolf rammed hard into the bag, its jaws digging into the leather.

An idea formed in his mind and Perry adjusted his grip on the satchel, wielding it like a shield. As long as he kept the durable hide between him and the wolf, he might have a chance at tiring the beast out enough to land a blow with the glass shard.

The wolf lunged again, its weight sending Perry stumbling, his back smacking against the trunk of a tree. The impact left him breathless for a moment. The wolf sensed his weakened state and lunged again. Perry barely got his saddlebag between them in time.

The wolf snapped its jaws in frustration, straining to get around the leather bag and into Perry's flesh. The creature had more stamina than Perry had suspected, and with his weapon-wielding arm pinned against the tree trunk, he couldn't move to attack the beast. He smelled its rancid breath as its teeth snapped within six inches of his face. Virtues, he wasn't going to best this beast.

The sound of hooves startled both Perry and the wolf. Had his mare rounded back for him?

"Perry!" a musical voice called, laced with fear.

Her voice filled him with both joy and terror. What was Jax doing all the way out here?

"Run, Jax!" Perry bellowed, still not seeing her anywhere. "Run! Wolves!" His strength was beginning to fail him, and the warning was all he could muster. She had to get away from here before the wolves descended upon her.

The white wolf dove for him again, this time, its fangs seizing the dangling strap of the saddlebag and yanking it away. The wolf had been smart, parting Perry from his last line of defense.

He held the broken mirror handle aloft, praying he could keep the wolf occupied long enough for Jax to getaway. He had to protect her at all costs. "Go, Jax. You must get out of here." His voice broke as the wolf crouched, preparing to launch itself at him for a final, lethal blow.

From behind Perry, branches crashed and the ground shook. A black stallion burst forth, heading straight for the white wolf. Atop the stallion sat a woman clutching a thin sword, its blade glinting with menace. The wolf jumped out of the way, but not before the blade came down on its thigh, red blood peppering the snow-covered ground.

The beast emitted a sharp whimper, backing away from the horse and its rider. Its predator gaze fell to Perry once more before it limped into the forest undergrowth and disappeared, leaving a trail of blood.

Relief overwhelmed Perry as he slumped against the tree trunk.

"Come quickly, dearest." Jax beckoned him to her horse. "That was only a flesh wound. He'll recover and be back with the pack."

Perry stared at her atop her mount, still brandishing her sword, slick with blood. Her caramel hair had come loose from its plait, flowing wildly behind her. She looked like a warrior goddess come to life.

"Are you hurt?" Her nose pinched with concern when he did not move. She made to lower herself from her horse, snapping Perry from his dazed state.

"No, no, I'm quite all right." They needed to get away from here before the pack returned seeking vengeance. He darted forward, snatching up his saddlebag and throwing it over his shoulder. He would have to send word to Master Gurns that his well-crafted bag had survived a wolf attack without so much as a single tear.

Jax held her hand out to him, ready to assist him onto her horse Mortimer's back. Her amethyst gaze, still wide with trepidation, flickered to his other hand as he reached for hers. He still clutched the glass mirror handle.

Perry tucked the useless trinket into the folds of his cloak and hoisted himself onto Mortimer's saddle.

Jax glanced at him over her shoulder. "Some Pettraudian wolf-fighting tradition I don't know about?" Her eyes twinkled.

At her jesting comment, he dissolved into heady laughter.

Chapter Seven

"When I returned from Lake Saltrine to find you gone, I tracked down Hendrie to see where you'd run off to," Jax explained a while later. Together, they sat curled up in front of the roaring fire that bathed Perry's sitting room in delicious heat. "He said you'd gone into Sephretta and taken one of the Ducal Guard as an escort." Her features contorted into a scowl. "Of course, when I asked George who had gone with you, we quickly found out that was *not* the case."

At her rebuke, Perry's cheeks warmed with shame. "You mustn't blame anyone but me, Jax. Corporal Highriver tried to assign me an escort, but…"

"Oh, don't worry, dearest. I'm not blaming anyone *but* you."

Perry glanced at Jax. She appeared to be struggling to keep a stern face, which touched his heart.

"I-I just wanted some time to myself," Perry said with a sigh. "It's quite tiring, having everyone think me an incompetent fool. I wanted to prove I was capable of doing such a simple task as retrieving your Yuletide gift all on my own." He stared down at his fingers entwined with Jax's. "But it turns out I couldn't even accomplish something as straightforward as that."

Jax frowned. "Who has made you feel like an incompetent fool?"

Perry gave her a dry look. "Who *hasn't* would be a much shorter list."

"I hope I am on the shorter list." She tenderly squeezed his hand. "Anyone who has done otherwise…well, I must say they aren't a very good judge of character, then."

"You're too kind to me, Jax." Perry shook his head with a sigh. "I'm inclined to think them right. Not only did I put myself in danger to appease my ego, but you as well." He held her gaze. "I can't believe you went searching for me."

Jax scoffed. "Well, I couldn't very well leave my future husband to the wolves, now could I?"

Her beautiful face became a bit blurry as tears came unbidden to his eyes.

"Mind you, I ruffled a few feathers with my heroic actions." Jax dusted off the sleeve of her gown. "I'm sure to get quite the lecture from both George and Jaquobie tonight at dinner."

Perry nodded, the lump in his throat preventing him from speaking his gratitude.

At his silence, Jax continued, appearing a bit nervous, "I mean, it only made sense for me to ride out and join in the search. I know the woods around the palace better than anyone. I've been exploring them for years and know how turned around one can get in a snowstorm. I, too, understand the need to seek solitude sometimes. Elusive as it may be for people in our positions." She shook her head. "And then to find you sparring with a giant wolf with only a sliver of glass as your weapon. The Ducal Guard will be talking about that for years, dearest. Not many go head-to-head with a great white wolf and last more than a few minutes." Jax trailed off, her expression dimming. "Thank the Virtues Mortimer and I arrived when we did.

To think what might have happened if we didn't…"

Perry straightened at her unspoken admission. "You would have missed me?"

Jax's features pinched with annoyance. "Well, of course, I would have missed you!"

Perry laughed at her indignation, his reaction making her seem to grow all the more irritated.

"What is so funny about that?" She bristled. "Is it wrong for me to be afraid of losing you?"

Perry sobered. "No, my darling, it's not wrong at all. I'm sorry for laughing." His emotions still felt all over the place in the aftermath of the wolf attack. "I suppose…well, this might sound ridiculous, but it's just hard for me to wrap my mind around the notion that someone could *actually* care whether I live or die."

Jax's expression crumpled. "Oh, Perry."

Her unbridled sympathy brought a small smile to his lips. He had shared with her bits and pieces of his former life in Pettraud. How his beloved late mother was the only member of his family who ever made him feel like he was worth something. But he couldn't bear to share with her just how awful his brothers and father had made him feel. How worthless. How pointless his existence was. He didn't blame Jax for not truly understanding just how greatly her simple acts of kindness toward him had affected his sense of self-worth.

She cradled his chin in the palm of her delicate hand. "You matter to me, Lord Percival Pettraud. A very great deal."

He took her hand and kissed it, unable to convey with words just how much she truly meant to him.

"So…" Jax said after a time. "You rode into Sephretta to collect my Yuletide gift?" Her voice was teasing and coy.

The smile she brought to his face was short-lived. "Indeed. Although, I'm afraid I've already ruined the surprise. And the gift." He motioned to the broken glass mirror lying on the nearby end table.

Jax glanced at the mirror before patting Perry's chest. "Nothing is ruined, my darling. You are alive and unscathed because of that trinket. For that reason, the mirror could not have been a better gift." She reached across him, grabbing the broken handle piece. "Besides, I think I might use this in my study for weighing down my never-ending stack of paperwork."

Perry chuckled at her ingenuity. "Now, there's an idea."

"Something beautiful to look at while I skim through my daily reports." Jax sighed, leaning her head against Perry's chest. "Just once I'd like to be able to read something for fun."

Her wistful comment stirred hope within his chest. "You know, I might have just the thing." He extracted himself from the sofa and the comforts of Jax's body pressed against his and hurried into his bedchamber. His saddlebag sat on the floor by his bureau. Perry lifted the flap and grabbed the burlap-wrapped item still within.

"What's this?" Jax sat up straight as he returned to her side.

Perry handed her the wrapping. "Just something to commemorate the *first* time you saved my life."

Her head tilted with curiosity as she unraveled the twine and pulled back the burlap cloth, revealing the leather-bound book he'd written for her. She didn't speak as she stroked the violet-dyed cover, her fingers circling the amethyst and emerald gemstones before opening to the first page.

"*A Feast Most Foul*," she whispered the book's title, more to herself than to Perry.

He watched, nervously wringing his hands as she flipped from page to page, lingering on the illustrations he'd painted himself.

"Is this really written about *me?*"

He was too anxious to do anything other than bob his head.

When she reached the end of the book, she closed the cover carefully and lifted her gaze, silent tears streaming freely down her cheeks. Before he could move to comfort her, she took his face in her hands and pulled him close, her soft, searching lips meeting his own.

"Perry." Breathless, Jax glowed with happy radiance when they finally broke their passionate embrace. "This is truly the most beautiful gift I have ever received."

Chapter Eight

"You look stunning, my dear," Perry whispered into Jax's ear as they waltzed across the floor.

Jax's warm breath flitted over his cheek. "I could say the same. Every woman in the room is practically undressing you with their eyes."

Heated pleasure ran the length of Perry's body as he savored her closeness. It was the first time all evening they'd had a moment together, and he was intent on cherishing every minute.

A joyous melody hummed from the strings of the minstrels' instruments, capturing the mood of the gala perfectly. The Saphirian throne room had been decorated from top to bottom with Yuletide cheer. Garlands hung from every beam and pillar. Fir and pine trees had been cut down and brought inside, carefully decorated with candles and holly berries. Red and green silk streamers had been strung across the cavernous ceiling. Never had Perry seen such a festive sight.

"Duchess Jacqueline," a familiar gravelly voice cut through the applause once the dance had finished.

Jax and Perry both turned to find a short, rotund man waddling toward them.

"Earl Graveire." Jax dipped her chin in greeting.

Perry recognized the name from his studies. In an effort to fully prepare for the gala, upon his return from Sephretta, Perry had spent several more hours holed up in the castle's library, researching as much as he could about Saphire and its noble houses. House Graveire oversaw a large estate on Saphire's southeastern border.

The earl struggled to bow, given his size. When he managed to get himself upright, he wheezed, "I just wanted to say that my wife and I are very much enjoying the festivities and are honored that one of the villages under our care was selected for the Yuletide bounty."

It clicked into place where Perry had heard his voice before. It had belonged to one of the passengers in the carriage he had come across yesterday during his fateful ride back from Sephretta.

Jax smiled demurely at the man's grandiose flattery. "I am thankful to the Virtues for filling my nets so generously."

Earl Graveire bobbed his head, his many chins quivering. "Indeed. Indeed. Now, is this the young lord from Pettraud?" His beady amber eyes turned to lance Perry with a shrewd stare.

Perry straightened his shoulders, not backing down. "Greetings, Earl Graveire. I hope the winter season has allowed you a nice respite from overseeing your legendary grain empire." From his research, Perry had learned the Graveire estate sourced half the realm's grain.

Earl Graveire's chest swelled even greater. "Legendary? Oh, I don't know about that."

"Nonsense." Perry summoned his most charming grin. "The tools and techniques you've implemented over the last decade have changed the trade for the better if you ask me."

Graveire rocked back and forth on his heels, a surprisingly deft move for the obese man. "Why, thank you, my lord. I'm happy to hear my agricultural practices are appreciated." Bidding the couple goodbye, he sauntered away with a bounce in his waddle.

"Why, Perry! You surprise me." Jax giggled. "I didn't think you were interested in Saphirian farming methods."

Perry shrugged. "I'm merely interested in Saphire and its people. Especially one, in particular." He winked at her.

"Well, your flattery will certainly go a long way." Jax snorted in the most unladylike manner. "Earl Graveire holds a great deal of influence over the High Lords. I'm sure he'll be singing your praises all night."

"I'm happy to hear that."

Jax tilted her head. "Why, may I ask?"

Perry was taken aback by the confusion lacing her question. "Well, I need to impress *all* the High Lords. I want them to approve of me. I wouldn't want you to be forced to break the arrangement our fathers made."

Jax went rigid beside him. "Excuse me?"

The fire in her eyes left his thoughts scrambling. "Well, I, uh—"

"Force *me* to do something? I am the Duchess of Saphire, Perry. No one forces me to do anything." Jax folded her arms, shirking away from his arm. "Especially something I have no desire to do."

Despite being pleased by her latter statement, Perry worked to backtrack his previous words. "Forgive me, Jax. I meant no offense. It's just that it's been stressed to me all week that I needed to impress these High Lords tonight in order for our relationship to continue. Jaquobie and the others—"

"Jaquobie?" Jax snapped, cutting him off for a second time. "What did Jaquobie tell you?"

Perry shrugged. "He told me that the High Lords could poison you against me if they thought I was unsuitable to be Saphire's Prince Consort."

"Curse that man!" Jax seethed, balling her fists at her side. "He had no right."

Now, Perry was the one confused.

"As if the High Lords have any idea what it takes to be my Prince Consort." Jax gazed out across the throne room, surveying the joyous activity swirling all around them. "I'm sorry you've been lured here under false pretenses, Perry. The High Lords are certainly free to give their opinion, but nothing could change the way I feel about you." She reached for his hand, wrapping it in hers. "The Duchess of Saphire has made her decision who her Prince Consort shall be, and she is, if nothing else, a woman of her word."

Her formal declaration brought him great joy mixed with a lingering sadness, as she reminded him that their relationship was, after all, forged from an agreement made between their fathers.

She pulled him closer, her palm cupping his cheek in a tender embrace. "I know a political pact brought us together, but I can't help but wonder if the Virtues skillfully orchestrated this entire thing so that our paths might cross. I feel certain, my love, that we were destined to be together."

The throne room faded away, and there was only her standing before him, clad in her shimmering emerald gown. An ode to him and Pettraud, he now realized. Not caring about the inquisitive eyes analyzing their every move, Perry stepped forward, closing the small gap between them with a fierce and fervent kiss. "Whether it be destiny or the Virtues, I am glad I have found my way to you. I love you, Jax. You make me happier than I ever thought possible."

She murmured her affections against his ear, her warm breath melting his insides. "And I love you."

He pulled her out to the middle of the dance floor once more, eager to share his happiness with all the gathered guests.

As he and Jax danced, Perry spied Hendrie and Uma in the crowd. His valet raised his glass toward Perry in good cheer before setting the drink down and escorting Uma out to the dance floor.

"Saphire certainly puts my memories of Pettraudian Yuletide celebrations to shame," Perry mused as he twirled Jax in his arms.

She smiled back at him, looking truly pleased. "I'm relieved to hear that. I so much wanted you to enjoy your first Yuletide away from home."

Perry pulled her close, dipped her toward the floor, and lowered his voice. "With you, Jax, I am home."

Murder is a royal affair.

Discover the Court of Mystery series on eBook, audio, & paperback.

The Court of Mystery series

The Ducal Detective
A Feast Most Foul
A Voyage of Vengeance
A Summit in Shadow
Throne of Threats
Paradise Plagued
Burdened Bloodline
Sovereign Sieged
Crown of Chaos
Harrowed Heir
Ravaged Reign
Innocence Imprisoned
Ardent Ascension
Eternal Empire

More Cozy Mysteries by Sarah

Trending Topic Mysteries
Glenmyre Whim Mysteries
Book Blogger Mysteries

www.saraheburr.com

Acknowledgments

A big thank you to Evan Grant for being my social media maven. An incredible thank you to Angelina Gennis for bringing the Realm of Virtues to life with her artistic magic. Thank you to Bettye Underwood for her editorial review.

A special thank you to Mihail Uvarov, the designer of the original series covers. Your depictions of Jax will always hold a special place in my heart.

Dedication

153

To my youngest fans, Charlie and Gigi

About the Author

Sarah E. Burr has been dreaming of being Nancy Drew since her small-town days in Appleton, Maine—but when corporate America didn't deliver any mysteries, she started writing her own! Now an award-winning author, Sarah pens the Book Blogger Mysteries, Court of Mystery series, and the fan-favorite Trending Topic Mysteries and Glenmyre Whim Mysteries. Her cozy crafting caper, *You Can't Candle the Truth,* was a 2022 finalist for both the NGIBA and Silver Falchion awards, while *#TagMe for Murder* was a 2024 NGIBA finalist for Best Click Lit Fiction.

A proud Sisters in Crime member, Sarah also runs BookstaBundles, a content creation service for authors. She co-hosts *It's Bookish Time TV*, a cozy web channel full of fun author interviews, and blogs for *Writers Who Kill*.

When not plotting her next whodunit, Sarah sings show tunes, plays video games with her husband, and takes long walks with her adorable pup, Eevee. Want free short stories and exclusive updates? Join her newsletter here: https://bit.ly/saraheburrbookssignup.